DEAD AND GONE

DEAD AND GONE

Norah McClintock

Cover photography by Evan Dion

Scholastic Canada Ltd.

Toronto New York London Auckland Sydney
Mexico City New Delhi Hong Kong Buenos Aires

Scholastic Canada Ltd.
604 King Street West, Toronto, Ontario M5V 1E1, Canada

Scholastic Inc.
557 Broadway, New York, NY 10012, USA

Scholastic Australia Pty Limited
PO Box 579, Gosford, NSW 2250, Australia

Scholastic New Zealand Limited
Private Bag 94407, Greenmount, Auckland, New Zealand

Scholastic Children's Books
Euston House, 24 Eversholt Street,
London NW1 1DB, UK

National Library of Canada Cataloguing in Publication

McClintock, Norah
Dead and gone / Norah McClintock.

(A Mike and Riel Mystery)
ISBN 0-439-96759-7

I. Title.

PS8575.C62D42 2004   jC813'.54   C2004-900875-7

8 7 6 5 4 3   Printed in Canada   06 07 08 09 10

CHAPTER ONE

"Look at it as a chance to make a positive contribution to society," Riel said after the judge gave me one hundred hours of community service for theft-under-five-thousand-dollars. And all for a box of cupcakes I took from a bakery delivery truck, but never even ate.

I could have got away with probation pure and simple — stay out of trouble and it's all good. No harm, no penalty. Could have, but didn't. Oh, no. Riel had to stick his nose into it. Had to give his opinion even though nobody asked for it. Had to talk to the judge, who turned out to be a friend of his from way back. Had to say he thought maybe a little positive reinforcement would be in order. Geeze, like he wasn't hammering the lesson — *life*'s lesson, he called it — into my head every day of my life.

"I look at it as a chance to lose out on making money because now I have to work for free at the community centre," I said.

"Remember that the next time you decide you want something for nothing," Riel said.

The deal was this: I reported to the community centre after supper most nights and every Saturday morning. While I was there, I was supposed to do whatever I was told — mop, empty garbage, set up rooms for meetings, whatever. It meant that I had to get my homework done right after school most days, which really cut into my social life, not that it exactly sizzled.

"If you pay attention and do what you're told," Riel said, "maybe at the end they'll give you a reference that'll help you get a job." He was like that — always pointing out the benefits of an honest day's work, when he wasn't telling you that a job well done was its own reward, or something like that.

* * *

Rebecca walked over to the community centre with me the first day.

"You realize I'm hardly going to be able to see you," I said. "When I'm not working, I'm going to have tons of homework to catch up on."

"Well," she said, "I guess we're just going to have to do our homework together."

Rebecca was easy to like. I guess you could say she was sort of my girlfriend even though I hadn't really kissed her. Not yet anyway.

I smiled at her, then turned and approached the reception desk and handed a letter to the woman behind the desk. She looked at it.

"You want to see Mr. Henderson," she said. She gave the letter back to me. "Down those stairs there." When she pointed, I saw she had those fake pasted-on fingernails. I don't know how women can stand wearing those things twenty-four hours a day, or even why they think they look good. They don't. They look like claws. "Take a left at the bottom," she said. "At the end of the hall there's a door that says Maintenance. If he's not there — " She shrugged. "He's around somewhere. He's the guy in blue workpants and a grey work shirt."

I glanced at Rebecca. She smiled and waggled her fingers at me in a little goodbye wave. I was on my own now.

I did a tour of practically the whole community centre before I found Mr. Henderson. He was around back, a guy with jet-black hair, standing just outside the door in work boots and a parka, watching a bunch of little girls learning to skate.

"Mr. Henderson?"

He nodded.

"I'm supposed to report to you," I said. I handed him the same piece of paper I'd showed to the woman at the reception desk.

He took it from me without shifting his eyes away from the rink, then turned and walked — *limped* — back to the door. It was a pretty bad limp. He tilted so far to the right with every step that I thought he would fall over, but then he would sort of kick his left leg forward and he'd look solid again. He reached the door, held the paper open under the light and read it. Then he handed it back to me.

"Come on then." He tugged open the door and led me up two flights of stairs to the top floor of the community centre. "You know how to mop a floor?" he said, reaching for a key ring that was attached to his belt. He unlocked the door to a small utility closet that had a sink in it, and a mop and a bucket on wheels, and a bunch of other cleaning supplies.

"Sure," I said. "Soap, water, mop. Right?"

Mr. Henderson didn't look impressed. "Bucket goes in the sink," he said, and waited until I got the point.

I heaved the bucket up into the sink and turned on the hot and cold water taps. Mr. Henderson reached across me and shut off the cold.

"Soap's there," he said, nodding to a big jug on the floor in the corner. "You put in a quarter of a cup."

I measured and poured. When the bucket was three-quarters full, he told me that was enough. Good thing — I almost got a hernia lifting the bucket out of the sink again. He took me out into the hall. He said that when I finished mopping each hallway, I should empty the dirty water and refill the bucket with clean hot water and another quarter cup of soap. "Don't walk back over the wet floor," he said, then, "Okay, let's see what you've got."

He watched me for a minute. Then he grabbed the mop from me and demonstrated what he called the proper technique. He handed me the mop and watched me again. He demonstrated two more times before he finally shook his head and muttered, "I guess that'll have to do." Geeze, and I thought Riel was fussy. "If you do the job right, it should take you an hour," he said. He started to limp away.

"Mr. Henderson?"

He turned slowly, like it was an effort. Everything about him was slow and deliberate — the way he had carefully read the paper I had handed him, the way he had climbed the stairs, the way he had watched me handle the mop before pulling it away from me and showing me the right way to hold it and move it.

"After I've finished here," I said, "then what?"

"If you've done it right, you go down to the second floor and mop that. If not, you do it over."

Terrific. "How do I know if I've done it right?"

His small brown eyes drilled into me, making me feel like I'd asked the world's stupidest question. "I'll tell you," he said.

* * *

I mopped the third floor of the community centre twice that night. When I told Rebecca about it the next day, she said, "Look on the bright side. You only had to do the second floor once." She grinned at me, her eyes amused, her copper hair like fire in the morning sun. I think that's what I liked about her. She always sounded like she was on my side.

Riel was like that too. He tried hard to make sure I knew he cared what happened to me. He worked at it when, really, how could I not know? If Riel didn't care, why would he have offered to take me in, to be a foster parent to me, when I had no place else to go? He wasn't related to me. I'd barely known him when I moved in with him. Sometimes I thought I still didn't know him all that well. He

5

was a serious guy. He worked hard at being a teacher, sitting at the dining room table almost every night, either preparing his lessons or grading tests and papers. He cooked supper almost every night too, and on the weekends he was teaching me to cook.

"It's something you need to know, Mike," he said, "so you don't end up eating junk food the rest of your life."

So far he'd showed me how to stuff and roast a small chicken, how to make black bean burritos with green chili, and how to throw together a sweet potato and mushroom casserole. I'd never admit it to him, but it was kind of fun.

After my first week at the community centre, Riel asked me how it was going.

"If you need a guy with a mop and a bucket, I'm your man," I said. "The guy I work for, Mr. Henderson, he could start The Church of How to Mop, he's that religious about it."

Riel said, "So I guess I can expect no more rush jobs with the kitchen floor or your bathroom."

Riel could start his own church: The Brethren of the Germophobes.

"I don't know," I said. "You heard of tennis elbow? I think I have mop elbow."

"That's all you do? Mop?" He sounded disappointed.

"Sometimes I get to sweep. I squeegeed some windows Wednesday night. Last night I got to set up tables in a room. Why?"

"I thought maybe they'd give you something more interesting to do. Maybe work with kids or something."

"By the time I'm done there, I'll have my cleaning technique nailed down," I said. "But interesting? I don't think so." I reached for the potatoes. "Mr. Henderson is a lot like you. Anything worth doing is worth doing right. If at first you don't do it the way he told you to, do it again."

"Sounds like a guy I could get along with."

I doubted it. Yeah, Mr. Henderson and Riel both seemed like they were into that cleanliness-godliness thing. Yeah, they were both serious. Yeah, they were both kind of quiet too. But with Riel, you got the idea he wasn't just into clean, he was into clean living. He worked hard. He got really excited about history and got a buzz from getting kids excited about it. The extent to which he kicked back: he had a beer. Sometimes he had it while he was making supper. Sometimes he had it after he had finished grading papers or preparing lessons or whatever he was doing. But that's all it was — one beer. Okay, if Susan came over — Dr. Susan Thomas, his girlfriend or maybe just his friend, I wasn't really clear on that and I hadn't got around to asking — he would open a bottle of wine and have a glass. And maybe he had a drink when he and Susan went out, I don't know. He didn't smoke. He didn't hang out in bars. He didn't do anything that made you think, okay, now I see where it is, the crack in that Mr. Clean image.

Mr. Henderson was different. Yeah, he waged the battle against dirt like he was a general, ordering me to attack first this front, then that one. Other than that, though, he and Riel had nothing in common. If Mr. Henderson was interested in anything except the war on grime, it was news to me. He hardly ever spoke — to me or anyone else. He was always in the background, working and watching what was going on at the community centre. Mostly he watched girls. He watched the little girls on the rink out back who were learning how to skate and do figures. He watched the high school girls who trooped in and out of step and yoga classes. He watched the girls who participated in swim meets at the community centre. Sometimes, like last night, he acted funny. While I was setting up chairs and tables in one of the big meeting rooms — something about a swim meet on Saturday — I spotted him in the hall outside the pool. He was standing by the door, looking at what was posted on the wall. When I went down there to ask him what he wanted me to do next, I saw he had his finger on one of the papers taped to the wall. He jerked it away when he saw me, like I'd caught him at something he wasn't supposed to be doing. But I couldn't see it on his face when he turned to me. Usually when you catch someone with their hand in the cookie jar, they have a guilty look on their face. But not Mr. Henderson. He looked the same as always, no expression you could read on his face, no expression in his dark brown eyes.

"You set up a hundred and twenty-five chairs?" he said.

I nodded.

"Five tables, three along the back, two up front?"

Geeze, like I was so stupid I couldn't have got that right. I nodded again.

"You put up the banner?"

Banner? "What banner? You never said anything about a banner."

"Wait here," he said. "I'll go get it."

While I waited, I glanced at the papers posted on the wall. They were lists of kids who were going to be in the swim meet — all girls. Mr. Henderson had been looking at lists of girls' names. See what I mean? I was pretty sure that if Riel met Mr. Henderson, they wouldn't hit it off. But it didn't seem likely that they would meet. Riel had his life and I had mine. And right now mine was long on grind and short on fun, thanks, mostly, to Riel, who had thought maybe they would give me something interesting to do for my community service order, maybe work with kids.

Someone hadn't done his homework before he stuck his nose into my business.

CHAPTER TWO

I had never hung around much at the community centre, but boy, it sure seemed like the rest of the world was there — all the time. There was something going on every night of the week. Boy Scouts and Girl Guides, karate club, dance socials for older people — much older people. Art classes, fitness classes — weights and step and kick boxing. A cooking club every other Tuesday for low-income mothers, where they cooked together and swapped recipes. Even a homework club for kids who wanted to do their homework together or who needed help but didn't have anyone at home who could give them a hand. And, of course, there was swimming. The community centre had a huge swimming pool and, besides classes, there were competitive and synchronized swim teams that practised regularly. Swim meets were held on a lot of Saturdays. There was always something going on. Always something to see.

Like girls in bathing suits. I like girls in bathing suits as much as any guy, I guess, which is one reason why, the first Saturday I worked at the community centre, I stopped and looked through the window that ran the whole length of the pool. There were dozens of girls in there — girls on the deck in bathing suits, most of them Speedos because they were racing, but looking great in them all the same, and girls on the bleachers, cheering on the teams from their schools. Catholic kids from an all-girls school. Some private-school girls too, which was the second reason I had stopped. My eyes swept the deck and the bleachers, wondering if Jen was there. She wasn't. The last reason I stopped: Mr. Henderson.

There's a wall of windows at one end of the third-floor corridor. From there you can look down on the pool. Mr. Henderson was up there, watching behind the glass. If it hadn't been for Thursday night, I might not have given him a second thought. It was a swim meet. You just naturally wanted to look and if there was a race just starting, you just naturally wanted to see who would win. You got involved.

But there was something about the way Mr. Henderson was watching, his hands pressed against the glass, staring hard at the girls down in the pool and around it. Today he was staring at one swimmer in particular. A blond girl who looked about my age. Slender, but not skinny. Strong-looking in her navy blue Speedo. She was twisting her pony tail up as she approached the racing platform at one end of the pool. She pulled on a bathing cap and stepped up onto platform number two and stood there, working her goggles down over her cap, looking back at some other girls in navy blue Speedos. Her teammates. She never once looked up to the third floor, never once saw Mr. Henderson watching her. If she had, she probably would have got mad. A guy my age gawking at her — and, okay, it was a good thing Rebecca wasn't there, because this girl

11

was really great looking — that was one thing. But an old guy like Mr. Henderson?

Then I thought about the list of names posted outside the pool. I thought about Mr. Henderson running his finger down that list, like maybe he'd been looking for someone. I wondered if it was the girl he was staring at now.

Eight girls stood on the racing platforms and adjusted their goggles. Eight girls crouched in a racing pose, ready to launch themselves into the water when the whistle blew. Eight girls, but there may as well have been only one as far as Mr. Henderson was concerned. His eyes never left the slender blond girl in the second lane as she flew forward, first in the air, then slicing through the water, then moving — boy, could she move! — down in her lane. Front crawl, right arm hooking up and then cutting into the water, left arm, right arm. She had a nice, steady stroke — even I could see that. She pulled out ahead of the other girls in the first few seconds and stayed out front, reaching the far end of the pool first, doing a little somersault-in-the-water turn and then heading back down the pool before anyone else did their turn. She won the race easily, to loud applause and shouts from one section of the bleachers — the girls from her own school.

I glanced up at Mr. Henderson. He watched her climb out of the pool. Watched her teammates surge around her, smiling, congratulating her. Watched her grin and turn and wave to the cheering section in the bleachers. Watched her walk across the deck and disappear through the door into the change room. Watched a few more seconds, his eyes on that door like maybe he was hoping she'd come back. But she didn't. Then, one after another, his hands came away from the glass. He straightened up and shook his head, the way you do when you're sort of dazed. Then he turned away. I waited a minute and then went back to work.

By the time I had finished mopping the hall, emptying my bucket and tidying the utility room, the swim meet was over. The girls were all filing into one of the big activity rooms where pizza and cookies and juice and pop had been set out. They chattered away like a flock of birds. Girls — they never seem to run out of stuff to talk about. Or laugh about either. They crowded into the room. The ones who had been swimming — you could tell which ones they were because most of them had damp hair, like they couldn't be bothered to dry it completely — all had backpacks, with their swim gear inside, I figured. They dropped their packs and coats near the door and headed straight for the pizza. The other girls, the ones who hadn't been in the pool, mostly went for the juice and the diet pop and maybe nibbled on a cookie.

I saw the blond girl drop her backpack on the top of the heap. She was with a group of girls, all damp-headed. Her hair was down over her shoulders now, which made her look even prettier. She and her friends headed right over to the boxes of pizza.

Then someone yelled.

Something crashed.

More people yelled.

There was an explosion of giggles.

Juice pooled on the floor, spreading out over broken glass. A couple of girls apologized over and over to one of the adults, a coach or a teacher, who was looking around, annoyed, for something to clean up the mess. I said I would take care of it. I ran down the hall to get my bucket and mop, a garbage bag and a pair of work gloves. By the time I got back, almost everyone had stepped away from the spill. One of the adults had squatted down and was picking up pieces of broken glass. She looked relieved to see me with my work gloves and mop.

"I'm sorry," she said.

I just shrugged. It was no big deal to me. I picked up the glass, most of it big pieces, and mopped up the juice. I was just getting the last of it, everybody pretty much ignoring me by then, all the girls eating and talking, all the adults relaxed now that the meet was over, when I looked over at the door. Mr. Henderson was there. He was holding a backpack and zipping up one of its pockets with one hand. It looked like the blond girl's backpack. He dropped it back onto the pile of stuff at the door and glanced around, like he was checking to see if anyone had seen him. I ducked my head and pretended to be engrossed in what I was doing. When I looked up again, he was gone.

One of the adults — a teacher, I think — clapped

her hands and called for everyone's attention. It took a while for the girls to settle down. But they finally did. They sat on the chairs that I had set out, all of them with their backs to the door. I trundled my bucket and mop across the room. I paused at the door, thinking about the blond girl and the way Mr. Henderson had been looking at her, thinking about him with her backpack, zipping up one of the pockets. Why had he been watching her? What had he been looking for? I glanced at the backpack sitting there at the top of the heap. Then I looked over my shoulder at the rows of chairs, each one with a girl in it, all of them looking in the opposite direction. They would never notice — at least, that's what I told myself. I turned a little, reached out and snagged the backpack. I held it in front of me where no one in the room could see it while I pushed my mop and bucket out into the hall. I shoved the bucket down the hall a few paces, then stopped and unzipped the pocket I had seen Mr. Henderson zipping up. The only thing in it was a shiny black leather wallet with a silver star dangling from the zipper. I glanced around, checking to make sure no one was watching me. The girls in the meeting room were clapping. A few were cheering. They were handing out the swim meet medals.

I opened the wallet. Whatever else Mr. Henderson had been doing, he hadn't been stealing from the girl. There were three twenties in the money compartment — *three!* — plus a ten and some fives. I was definitely doing something wrong with my life. It was like every girl I ever ran into had way more money than me. The wallet also had a zippered compartment and a bunch of slots where you could put credit cards or ID cards. There were two cards in the slots: a student transit pass and a SAC card. Each card had the girl's name on it — Emily Corwin. She went to Holy Name Girls' School. She was in grade nine, which surprised me because she looked older. Especially, it turned out, when she was mad.

"What do you think you're doing?" she said, startling me just as I was fiddling with the zippered compartment. "That's mine!"

She had come out of nowhere — she must have used transporter technology to get there because she hadn't made any noise at all. She reached out, grabbed the dangling silver star, and jerked the wallet away from me. She grabbed the backpack from me too. "I'm telling," she said. She sounded like she was in grade two now instead of grade nine.

"It's all there," I said. Part of me wanted to smile, to show her how harmless I was. But she might be the kind of girl who would mistake a smile for a smirk, who might think I was trying to put one over on her, and then she'd tell for sure. And if there was one thing I didn't need, it was more trouble. Let the word get back to Riel that I had been caught going through a girl's wallet and I'd probably be grounded for life.

"I didn't take anything," I said. "Honest."

"Honest?" she said. "You've got to be kidding." She held out the wallet, which she was still holding by the silver star. "Open it," she said. "Show me."

Anything to keep her from yelling for a teacher.

I unzipped the wallet again and held it open, showing her the ID cards.

"What about the money?" she said.

I held open the money compartment.

"Take it out," she said. She had a bossy way of talking, but then, why not? She had the upper hand. "Show me."

I took out the three twenties and the ten and what turned out to be three fives. Almost a hundred dollars.

"Okay," she said. "Put everything back and zip it up again."

When I handed the wallet to her, she took it by the star again and twirled it while she looked at me. The way she was standing, she seemed a little more relaxed, but her face was still hard and suspicious.

"See?" I said. "It's all there."

"For all I know, that's only because you didn't have time to take it. If I hadn't spotted you on my way to the stage, maybe you would have stolen the money, put the wallet back and taken off."

My life was starting to flash before my eyes. Geeze, I should have just left it alone. I should never have touched her stuff, because the way it looked, Emily Corwin was going to tell on me. She was going to run into the room, find a coach or a

17

teacher, and she was going to report me. For sure whoever she complained to would turn around and complain to the director of the community centre, who knew I was here on a community service order and who would turn around and complain to my youth worker, who would tell Riel. I should definitely have left it alone.

"It's not what it looks like," I said.

"Really? So you have some reason to be going through my wallet besides the eighty-five dollars in it?"

She had light honey-coloured hair, but dark chocolate eyes. I stared into those eyes and tried to decide which way to push the conversation. One, I could tell her the truth — that Mr. Henderson had been watching her, that he'd gone through her stuff first. But she'd probably think I was laying it off on someone else, on some old geezer no one had even noticed. And anyway, Mr. Henderson had been here longer than me. He was an adult. They were paying him. He wasn't here on a community service order. So who would they believe when he denied doing it? And I was pretty sure he would deny it, because no matter how long he'd been there, it wouldn't look good, an old guy like him going through some girl's backpack. Which led me to, Two: I could give her another reason for going into her stuff, one she might actually believe.

"I saw you swim," I said. "You're good." She had her arms crossed over her chest now, listening, maybe even interested. But I could see she wasn't going to be an easy sell. "You were way out front right from the start. No one else had a chance against you."

And there it was, like the first glint of spring on a solid-frozen lake — she started to thaw just a little.

"You swim?" she said. She looked me over, like she was wondering, did I have the right kind of body for a swimmer.

"Just barely," I said. "But my best friend Sal was on the swim team at my school. I used to go to the meets — you know, cheer him on."

"Sal's a *guy*'s name?" she said.

So I told her that Sal was short for Salvatore, and where Sal was from, and that he had won the city championships in his division last year in freestyle and in butterfly. That impressed her.

"Butterfly's tough," she said.

I thought of offering to fix her up with Sal. Maybe that would make her forget she had found me going through her wallet. But with girls, you never know. Something like that might be just the thing to make a problem go away, or it might set her off, get her all insulted and mad-looking again. So instead I said, "I bet you do a good butterfly too, the way you move doing the crawl."

"I do an okay butterfly," she said, and I had the feeling she was being honest, not just modest. "But the freestyle's my specialty. What school do you go to?" When I told her, she said, "Yeah, they're good. The boys' team is better than the girls' team, though."

Okay. If she said so.

She looked down at her wallet, which she was still dangling by the chain.

"Were you trying to steal from me?" she said.

"I just wanted to see who you were." I gave her a bit of a smile, one that I hoped conveyed the idea that I thought she was kind of cute.

She seemed to consider my answer. "You couldn't just come up to me and ask?"

I looked at the door to the activity room. I heard clapping again.

"There are a hundred and twenty-five girls in there," I said.

"More like a hundred," she said, "plus teachers and parents and coaches." She smiled, not a full-force, all-out megawatt smile, but at least she didn't look like she was ready to turn me in anymore. "My name is Emily," she said. "Emily Corwin."

"I know," I said, nodding at the wallet. I told her my name.

"Emily!" someone called from the door to the activity room. "Come on."

Emily looked at me for a few seconds and then shrugged. "See you around," she said. "Maybe."

"Yeah," I said. Mostly I was thinking, never again. Never again would I do something that stupid, something that could land me in big trouble. It wasn't worth the stress.

She walked away, her backpack slung over one shoulder, the wallet still dangling from her fingers.

I watched her until she went back inside, then I waited a few more minutes to see if anyone was going to come rushing out, ready to report me. No one did. As I pushed my bucket down to the utility room and emptied it, I told myself that was the end of it. I rinsed and wrung out my mop. Then, I couldn't help myself, I went back to the pool and looked at the lists of names that were posted on the wall. There were three of them. When I'd seen Mr. Henderson, he'd had his finger on the middle one. I looked at it now. There, near the top of the page, was her name: *Corwin, Emily*.

* * *

"You think it's weird that an old guy is always looking at girls?" I said.

Riel glanced at me for maybe a nanosecond before turning his attention back to the TV.

"In a minute, Mike, okay?" he said.

I waited, half listening to what they were saying on TV.

"What was that all about?" I said when he finally hit the off button on the remote. "They found a body?"

"They found some bones," Riel said. "The guy who found them, a guy who was out hiking in the woods, called the police because he thought they might be human bones."

"And are they?"

"Looks like it," Riel said.

I'd got dragged on a couple of hikes last year at school. The first time I ended up with a blister on my heel. The second time it started to pour halfway through and I got drenched. Both times we were supposed to keep our eyes open for certain things — birds, birds' nests, garter snakes, evidence of beaver activity. Mostly it was a big yawn. We didn't see anything even half as interesting as human bones.

"So, what does that mean?" I said. "Some guy — or maybe it was a woman — was murdered out in the woods and buried in a shallow grave?" For some reason, whenever they found a body out in the woods, it was always in a shallow grave. I used to wonder why that was. Then I decided that the really smart killers, the ones who didn't want their victims to be found, probably put a little extra effort into it and dug deeper graves.

"Nobody said anything about a grave, shallow or otherwise," Riel said. He was very big on accuracy. Almost as big as he was on cleanliness and tidiness. "Nobody said anything about murder, either."

"Yeah, but they found bones — "

"There are lots of reasons why you might find bones in the woods," Riel said.

"*Human* bones?" I said.

"Could be they came from an aboriginal burial ground in the vicinity."

"Is there an aboriginal burial ground in the vicinity?" I said.

"Not that I know of."

Score one for Mike, for a change.

"Could be they belong to someone who settled up

22

there a hundred and fifty or more years ago," he said. "Someone who died and was buried. And maybe wild animals got to the grave, scattered the bones."

"Maybe someone who settled up there a hundred and fifty or more years ago was murdered," I said.

"It's possible."

A-ha! "So what are they going to do?"

"The police?" He shrugged, like it was no big deal, like he hadn't been sitting there glued to the TV, watching hard enough to get every detail. But once a cop, always a cop. Riel still took a big interest in the crime section of the newspaper and the crime stories on radio and TV. "They've already called in a forensic anthropologist who's confirmed that they're human bones. The next step is for the anthropologist to date the bones and tell the police whether they're a couple of years old or a couple of hundred years old."

"And how the person died?"

"Depends," Riel said.

"On?"

"On *how* the person died. And on the state of the remains. A person who maybe had a heart attack and all that's left is bones, I'm not sure they'll be able to say for sure how that person died."

"But a person's whose head was maybe sawed off — "

"Geeze, Mike."

"Or maybe hacked off. You know, maybe a hundred and fifty or more years ago."

"Well, then it wouldn't matter, would it?" Riel said. "Whoever might have done it would be in a shallow grave of his own by now, right? So," changing the subject, "what's this about an old guy looking at girls?"

"The guy I work for, he's an old guy, older than you."

"That old, huh?" He sounded partly amused, partly not-so-amused.

"And he's always checking out the girls at the community centre."

"What do you mean, checking them out?"

"Looking at them. Watching the girls' skating lessons. Watching the swim meets."

Riel leaned forward. "And?"

"And what?"

"You asked me if I thought it was weird. Do *you* think it's weird?"

"I don't know," I said. I couldn't decide. "I mean, he works there. Maybe he's just interested. Maybe he has kids of his own." I didn't know anything about him. "But there's this one girl — I saw him look in her backpack when she wasn't there."

Riel leaned forward a little more. "Did he take anything?"

"No."

"Did you report it?"

"Well, no."

"Don't you think you should?"

"Well, I guess, but . . . " But if I did, Mr. Henderson would deny it. And Emily wouldn't be able to back me up because I had lied about why I had gone into her backpack, which was a whole area I didn't want to get into with Riel.

"Talk to Teresa." Teresa Rego, director of the community centre. "She's a good person. She'll know what to do."

"Yeah, but — "

"Do the right thing, Mike."

The phone rang.

"You done your bathroom yet?" Riel said, moving to answer it.

"Not yet." Geeze, I'd just got home.

"How about it, then? Get it done before supper," he said, reaching for the receiver, picking it up, saying "Hi," and then smiling. I knew that smile. It had to be Susan. "Just a sec," he said. He covered the mouthpiece with one hand. "Get your bathroom done, then maybe call Sal. See if he wants to come over. You can order a pizza. I'll give you money to rent a video. What do you say?"

"Going out with Susan, huh?"

There it was, that smile again.

CHAPTER THREE

"It says here maybe six or seven years," I said. I held the newspaper out to Riel. "Those bones? It says they belong to a guy and they've been out there maybe six or seven years, that's all. It also says the cops — "

He gave me that sharp look. Geeze.

"The *police*," I said, "are looking for the rest of him. How do they know from a couple of bones that it's a guy?"

"Depends on what they found," Riel said. He took the paper from me and reached around me with his other hand for the coffee pot. The coffee he drank was grown in the rainforest and he poured organic milk into it, but it gave him a major hit of caffeine all the same. "With some bones, the pelvis, I think, and the skull, you can tell male from female pretty easily — if you know what you're doing."

In that case, either it wasn't a skull or a pelvis, or someone didn't know what he was doing, because it had taken them almost a whole week to figure it out. Or, maybe, to get around to figuring it out.

"You think you can handle things around here after school?" Riel said. "Get yourself something to eat, then get to the community centre on time?"

Thanks for the vote of confidence. "I have a perfect record so far," I said. "You can ask Mr. Henderson. I've never been late. Why?"

"Susan has this thing she wants me to go to."

"What kind of thing?"

"A fundraising thing."

"Yeah? What for?"

What was that I saw in his eyes? Embarrassment? Must have been, because his cheeks turned a little pink.

"Come on, what for?" I said.

"The ballet." His voice was gruff, like he was daring me to call him on it.

"You're going to the *ballet*?" I tried to imagine it. Riel was a guy who mostly dressed casual, mostly black jeans or a pair of charcoal slacks he liked, although I had seen him put on a suit from time to time when he was going somewhere with Susan. He was a sports-outdoors kind of guy. It was hard to picture him watching girls in tutus and guys in tights prancing across a stage.

"Susan likes the ballet," he said, as if that explained everything.

I thought about the girls I had known — all two of them, Jen and now Rebecca — and what I would have done for them if I cared enough.

"I'll be fine," I said.

* * *

Sal came by while I was microwaving the chicken quesadilla Riel had left for me.

"What's up?" I said.

"Nothing."

He looked tired. It was his natural state these days. Sal's dad was sick. He'd been in the hospital — psych ward — for over a month and now he was home and on serious medication. He sat in the living room when he wasn't in bed. Half the time, Sal said, he just stared out the window. The rest of the time he read poetry in Spanish. Back in Guatemala, where Sal is from, his father had been a professor at a university. He taught poetry. When they came here, though, the only job he could get was as a cleaner in a downtown office building. And now he couldn't even do that. Sal's mom worked, but she didn't have the world's greatest job. So Sal had had to get a job to help pay the bills. He put in thirty hours a week at the McDonald's on Danforth, and that was on top of school.

"You working tonight?" I said.

"Eight o'clock."

The microwave buzzer went off. "You hungry?" I said. "You want some of this?"

He shook his head. I felt bad eating in front of him, though, so I gave him a Coke. He drank it. While I ate, I told him about Emily and how she thought the swim team at our school was pretty good.

"She's pretty, too," I said. "And I told her about how you won the city championships last year." He winced. Sal had really liked being on the team. He'd hated it when he had to quit. "Hey, you want to meet her? I think they're practising at the community centre tonight."

He shook his head.

"Come on," I said. "She's rich."

It was the wrong thing to say. Not only did Sal

have to work to help out his family, but his family also rented out half of their tiny house. They had to, to afford the rent. Sal's shoulders slumped.

"Why would a rich girl be interested in me?" he said.

"Jen was interested in me," I said.

He looked at me and I knew which word he had zeroed in on. *Was*. And, anyway, Sal had never had a high opinion of Jen. Rich girls, he said, they think the whole world revolves around them. He said Jen was walking proof of that.

"This one's different," I said. I told him how I'd met her. "Anyone else would have screamed for the cops, but she didn't. She turned out to be okay."

"Yeah?" Sal said. He still wasn't impressed. "Maybe *you* should ask her out."

"It's not like that," I said. I was going with Rebecca and that suited me just fine. Rebecca wasn't rich, but she was cool. Maybe the coolest girl I had ever met. "I thought you might be interested, that's all. You two have something in common. You could talk about swimming, see where it goes from there."

He said no, he didn't have time for a social life these days, not with school full time and working full time. "But I'll walk over there with you," he said.

I cleaned up the kitchen and we headed for the community centre. We were half a block away when we heard them. Girls. Talking, giggling, shrieking, making that high-pitched jumble of girl noises.

Then we saw them, a whole crowd of them, coming out the front door of the community centre, heading for the sidewalk. They stopped when they got there and talked back and forth for a few minutes before fanning out, some heading east, some heading west, some heading north to the subway.

"That's her," I said. "The girl I was telling you about. See, the blond in the light blue jacket."

Sal turned his head to look, but I think he only did it for me — not because he was interested, but because I was working so hard to cheer him up. But, boy, he didn't keep on looking because of me. When he focused in on Emily, his eyes almost came out of his head. For what seemed like the first time since his dad had got sick, he smiled.

"See what I mean?" I said.

He didn't answer. He just kept staring at her.

"Come on," I said. I grabbed him by the arm. He jerked free of me.

"Uh-uh," he said.

"You'd like her," I said. I was sure of it, now that I saw the look on his face. "I told you, she's a swimmer. She thinks our school's team is pretty good. And when I told her about you, she looked interested."

"No," he said.

Geeze, if I had something in common with someone like Emily and someone was offering to introduce me — and if I didn't already have a girlfriend — I'd be sprinting across the street. "Why not?"

"I just don't want to, okay?" Sal said. He sounded angry now.

"Yeah, but — "

"No," he said. "Look, I gotta go."

He spun around and took off in the opposite direction from the community centre. I was going to go after him. I had a couple more minutes before I had to be at work and I didn't want him to walk away angry. Besides, Emily and another girl were on the other side of the street now, heading north. So I turned to chase Sal. That's when I saw Mr. Henderson. He was crossing the street Emily and her friend had just crossed. Maybe he was going up to the store on the corner to get something. That's probably what I would have assumed if I hadn't seen him checking out Emily at the swim meet, if I hadn't seen him reading the list of participants, his finger resting where Emily's name was.

I glanced at my watch. Another two minutes and I'd be late. But the person I was supposed to check in with was Mr. Henderson. And he wasn't at the community centre. He was walking up the street behind Emily. Maybe *following* Emily.

I joined the parade.

I was careful to hang back almost a full block. It's a good thing it was dark. I could keep an eye on Mr. Henderson and, up ahead, on Emily, and if either of them turned around, I could duck behind one of the big trees that lined the street or I could turn up a walkway to one of the houses and they probably wouldn't recognize me.

Neither of them turned. Emily was telling her friend something. At least, that's what it looked like. I couldn't hear what either of them was saying, but Emily was a hand-talker. She kept throwing up her arms and flinging out her hands. Maybe she was making a point or maybe she was demonstrating some swim move to her friend, I wasn't sure which. They passed a corner store a couple of blocks north of the community centre and a couple of blocks south of Danforth Avenue, where the subway station was. Then Mr. Henderson passed it. I kept on his tail.

Emily and her friend reached Danforth and crossed at the light. The light had changed from green to yellow to red by the time Mr. Henderson got there. I watched him stand on the sidewalk for a moment. Emily and her friend must have turned off somewhere because I couldn't see them anymore. Then Mr. Henderson darted across the street against the light. For a guy with a limp, he could move pretty fast when he wanted to. I jogged up to the corner.

Emily and her friend must have gone into the subway because that's where I saw Mr. Henderson go. From where I was standing on the corner, I could see him in the bright light. He was right between the ticket taker and the turnstiles, looking toward the escalator. Then, just like that, he turned and came back out, limping heavily on his right side and then kicking out his left foot, moving fast toward the corner and the streetlight. I turned and jogged down the way I'd come. I didn't look back. I just kept moving until I pushed my way through the door to the community centre. I raced up to the third floor and found the utility closet door propped open, which surprised me. Mr. Henderson took his responsibilities seriously, which meant that he kept everything locked and kept a close hold on the keys. Usually I had to get him to open the door for me, using a key on the chain that was attached to his belt. When I was on a floor, I kept the door propped open — you had to, just in case it accidentally closed and locked.

I was filling my bucket when I heard Mr. Henderson coming down the hall. You couldn't miss him, not with that *shuffle-thump* way of walking he had. Then I could feel him behind me. When I turned around, I made myself think about Sal, about Rebecca, about anyone except Emily, because if I thought about her, I'd probably end up looking guilty.

"You sure you know what you're doing?" Mr. Henderson said.

The question threw me. Had he seen me following him? Is that why he was asking?

"Yeah," I said. "Third floor, then second floor, then first, right?" Like I did every night. "Unless there's something else you want me to do."

He shook his head.

"I'll check on you," he said. Check on my work, he meant.

While I mopped, I wondered why he had been following Emily. He had gone into her wallet. So had I. Apart from some money and a couple of student

ID's, there was nothing there. Nothing except her name and the name of her school.

Not even an address, I thought.

Was that what he was looking for, her address? No, that couldn't be it. He knew her name. If he wanted to know where she lived, all he had to do was look in the phone book — didn't he?

I mopped the third floor.

I mopped the second floor.

I mopped half of the first floor and stopped when I reached the pay phone in the main corridor. There was a telephone directory chained to the wall under it. I left my mop in the bucket, pulled out the directory and flipped through it. *C. . . . Co . . . Cor . . . Cornwall . . . Corsetti . . . Corvo . . . Cory . . .* Wait a minute. *W* comes after *V* and before *Y*. I looked again. There were no Corwins in the phone book. Emily was unlisted.

* * *

Earthquakes, avalanches, tornadoes, floods — those are all things that happen somewhere else, to someone else. They're things I've never paid much attention to, other than seeing them on the news. Same with fires.

Sure, we had fire drills at school a couple of times a year. And a couple of times a year someone set off the alarm — it was always supposed to be a joke, but Mr. Gianneris never thought it was funny. If he caught who did it, the kid(s) got a three-day suspension. And one of the first things Riel had showed me when I moved in with him was where he kept the fire extinguisher. Riel is that kind of guy — like a boy scout. Always prepared. But I'd managed to get through life without ever actually having to deal with a fire. I thought the chances I would ever have to deal with one were about zero.

I smelled it first. I was sweeping the halls on the third floor of the old, original wing of the community centre. My first thought: someone is smoking. That's a big no-no. The community centre is a smoke-free zone. The smell seemed to be coming from the end of the hall, in or near the big room that everyone called the studio because it was where art classes were held. And, boy, was that going to get someone in trouble, because there was a lot of stuff in there — solvents and rags and paper — that could really go up if there was a fire.

Then I heard a bell. A fire alarm. When the fire alarm sounded at school, the teachers made sure everyone got up and left the school. This was supposed to be done in what Mr. Gianneris called "an orderly fashion." It was also supposed to be done immediately. The school checked later to see if it was a real fire or not. Better safe than sorry, Mr. Gianneris always said.

At the community centre it was different. The alarm went off. Doors opened and people stuck their heads out into the corridor where I was sweeping. You could see they were all wondering — is it real? Do I have to leave the building? You could also see that nobody really wanted to. It was cold outside. If it was a false alarm, they'd have to stand out there shivering until the fire department sounded the all-clear. A lot of heads looked at me, I guess because I was out in the hall already.

I went down the hall to the studio. The smoke was definitely coming from there. I looked around. And then I did something stupid.

It turns out that pretty much the last thing you want to do when you follow the smell of smoke to a closed door is to fling that door open. You're supposed to be really careful because (it turns out) you have no way of knowing whether the fire behind the door is big or small. Also, when you open the door, it can cause a draft, which can make the fire worse. Fast. An open door (it turns out) also allows fire and smoke to spread.

But I didn't know that, so I opened the door — and immediately jumped back. Geeze, even if it had started out that way, what I had smelled wasn't a cigarette left in an ashtray. It wasn't even a match tossed into a wastepaper basket. What I had smelled was a major big deal fire that all of a sudden got bigger. I felt the heat — it came at me in a wave, blasting my face, pushing me back and further away from the door. Suddenly there was smoke everywhere, swirling around me and then spreading out into the hall. I heard people behind me now, all of them hurrying away from me and toward the stairs. The alarm was still ringing. I looked up at the ceiling. There were sprinklers up there, but they looked old and they hadn't come on yet.

"Hey!" someone called from the end of the hall. "Hey, get out of there!" It was Mr. Henderson. He was standing near the stairs. As far as I could tell, everyone else had left. "Come on," he shouted at me. "The fire department is on its way."

Nobody needed to tell me twice. I turned. Then, as fire engine sirens whoop-whooped outside, I heard something. A cry. I turned back to the studio, shaking my head — and I heard it again.

"You, Mike!" Mr. Henderson shouted from the end of the hall. "Come on! Out of the building." He sounded angry now.

"There's someone in there," I said. I couldn't see whoever it was. The fire was too big. The smoke was too thick.

Mr. Henderson thumped down the hall toward me. When he got to the studio door, he shoved me aside. "Hey!" he called. "Hey, is someone in there?"

"Help!" a panicked voice came from inside. "I can't get out."

Mr. Henderson slipped the straps of his overalls off his shoulders and peeled off his shirt. He tossed it to me. "The water fountain," he said. "Drench this. Now."

I raced down the hall, put the shirt in the fountain and pressed the button.

"Come on, come on," Mr. Henderson said.

I raced back and thrust the soaking shirt at him. "Go find the firemen," he said. "Now!" Then he plunged into the room, right through the fire and the smoke. I hung in the hallway for a moment, stunned, wondering if I'd ever see him again.

Then I turned and ran.

Firefighters were swarming into the building by the time I reached the ground floor. I grabbed the closest one and told him where the fire was, where Mr. Henderson was and what he was doing. He told me to go outside. I watched the firefighters head for the stairs. And then I saw Mr. Henderson. He was coming down the stairs. Staggering down them, actually. His face was dark and smoky looking and he was carrying a kid. A boy, maybe nine or ten years old. The kid was clinging to him. One of the firefighters took the kid from Mr. Henderson. The rest of them pushed by him and hurried up the stairs. The kid was coughing and blubbering when the firefighter carried him past me.

Mr. Henderson limped down the hall toward me, coughing. "The kid," he said. "He sneaked some cigarettes from his big sister's purse. Thought he'd give smoking a try. In the *art* room." He shook his head like he couldn't believe it. "One more way cigarettes can kill, huh?"

I stared at Mr. Henderson.

"You okay?" he said. "You're not hurt or anything, are you?"

Hurt? I shook my head. No, I wasn't hurt. But I was distracted — by the fact that brown-eyed Mr. Henderson now had one brown eye and one very blue one.

CHAPTER FOUR

It turned out the kid who had accidentally started the fire stuck around after it had started because he thought he could put it out and then slip out of the building before anyone noticed anything. It was a plan. It just wasn't a good one.

One of the firefighters questioned me about what I had seen and what I had done. I told him. That's when I found out that opening the door the way I did had been the wrong thing to do. "Next time," he said, "just clear the building. Let us worry about the rest."

Next time? Once in a lifetime was enough, thanks anyway.

Riel wasn't home when I got there. He'd left a note: Back by suppertime. I called his cell phone and reminded him that I had plans. Rebecca had invited me over. Her parents were going to a dinner party. She was going to make supper for me and then we were going to watch videos.

"Don't do anything I wouldn't do," Riel said. Then, "You know about the birds and the bees, right, Mike?"

The birds and the bees? "You mean human reproduction?" I said.

Silence for a second. Then, "Yeah."

Geeze. "We're having supper, then we're going to watch videos," I said, in case he hadn't heard me right the first time.

More silence. It seemed different this time, though, like maybe he was relieved. "Be good," he said. "And be home by midnight, okay?"

* * *

Rebecca lived a few blocks from Riel in a house that her father, a real handy guy, had expanded and renovated. It was nice. Everything at Rebecca's house was nice. Her mother was an art teacher at a private girls' school. All the walls at Rebecca's house were painted bright colours and there were lots of pictures hanging on them. The best part, though, was the solarium her dad had added to the back of the house. You could sit out there summer and winter and look at the sky and the grass or the snow, whatever season it happened to be. We ate in the solarium that night at a little round table Rebecca had set with what she said were her mother's best dishes. She put a candle in the middle of the table and dimmed the lights. The flame from the candle lit up her coppery hair, making it almost red in some places, pure gold in others. She looked great. She was also a good cook. She made spaghetti with little meatballs, garlic bread and a salad. After we ate, I helped her carry everything back into the kitchen. I wanted to help her clean up, too, but she was nervous about her mother's dishes, so she washed and dried, and I just stood around and watched. That's when I told her about Mr. Henderson.

"He sounds creepy," she said. "Did you tell Mr. Riel?"

She called him *Mister* because he was her history teacher. She got kind of tense whenever she was around him, for the same reason. I kept telling her he was a nice guy. I had the impression she already knew that, but she couldn't get past the fact that he assigned her homework and graded her tests, and once, when she wasn't prepared for class, he had told her he was surprised that someone like her had slacked off. What do you think he meant, someone like me? she had asked me. Does he mean he thinks I should never slack off because I'm not smart? Her average in his class was eighty-three. I told her that for sure Riel thought she was smart, but that he expected smart people to *act* smart. Acting smart, I told her, was showing up on time, doing your work, and always being prepared.

"He said I should report it to the director of the community centre," I said.

"Did you?"

"I feel funny about it," I said. "I mean, what am I going to say? I saw Mr. Henderson go through a girl's backpack? He's just going to deny it. And, besides, he didn't take anything."

"Maybe not this time," Rebecca said. "But what if he does it again?"

I knew she was right, the same as I knew Riel was right. But I had already messed up by going into Emily's backpack myself — and getting caught. If I told Teresa Rego what I had seen, she would probably want to check with Emily to make sure that nothing was missing, and then Emily would say that she saw *me*, not Mr. Henderson, looking not only in her backpack but in her wallet. She'd say I never even mentioned Mr. Henderson. Geeze, I never should have touched her stuff. I never should have lied about it. I never should have mentioned Mr. Henderson to Riel. Or to Rebecca. Except that there was something not right about it all.

"You should at least talk to the girl," Rebecca said. "Tell her what happened."

"You mean just walk up to her and say, Excuse me, Emily, but the janitor at the community centre seems to have a thing for you?"

"Emily?" Rebecca said. "So you know this girl?"

"I talked to her once."

"Oh?"

That's all she said. *Oh.* Then she gave me a look and the next thing I knew I was telling her everything — that I had gone into Emily's backpack myself, that she'd caught me looking through her wallet.

"She was kind of snotty at first," I said, "but by the end she was okay. She didn't report me."

"Because you told her you wanted to find out who she was," Rebecca said. "Because you told her you were interested in her." She was still giving me that look.

"I only said that because she thought I was trying to steal from her."

"It never occurred to you to tell her the truth? It never occurred to you to say what you saw Mr. Henderson do?"

"I thought she would think I was lying."

"So, instead, you lied to her?"

"No." Geeze, it wasn't like that. Except that it was, sort of. "Mr. Henderson would have denied it. And I have a record. The only reason I'm at the community centre is because I took something."

Rebecca rolled her eyes. "Who is this Emily anyway?" she said. "Does she go to our school?"

I shook my head. "Her name is Emily Corwin. She goes to private school."

"Corwin? Emily *Corwin*?"

"Yeah." The look she was giving me now was scarier than the one she had given me before. "Why? Do you know her?"

"Emily Corwin with long blond hair, kind of skinny?"

"I don't know about skinny, but she looks good in a bathing suit." I regretted the words as soon as I had said them. Rebecca crossed her arms over her chest and gave me a sharp look. "The first time I saw her was at a swim meet," I said. "And, anyway, it was a Speedo bathing suit."

"Instead of, say, a thong bikini?" Rebecca said.

Geeze, that wasn't what I meant at all. "Besides, she's only in grade nine."

"A whole year behind you, you mean," Rebecca said. "If only she was in grade ten and had been wearing a thong bikini."

"I'm not interested in her," I said. Then I said, "How do you know her anyway?"

"How do I know Emily Corwin who you're not

interested in even though you told her you were interested?"

I should have been a miner — or maybe a gravedigger — because I was shovelling myself in deeper and deeper. So I did the only thing I could think of — I took the dishtowel out of Rebecca's hand and folded it over the towel rack. Then I kissed her. For the first time. And while I was doing it, while I was feeling her lips and smelling how fresh and clean she was, I wondered why it had taken me so long, why I hadn't done it before.

Rebecca put her arms around my waist and leaned forward and kissed me back. When she pulled away, which she did just a little, she was smiling.

"I knew you'd be a good kisser," she said. She smiled. "I'm sorry. I guess I came across sounding jealous."

"That's okay." I'd never had a girl be jealous because of me before.

"She's a year behind because she had some kind of family problem."

"Emily?"

"Yeah, Emily. She's the same age as you and me, but she missed a year at school. I know her from junior high. I was on the basketball team at my school." Rebecca is tall for a girl. Almost as tall as me. "We played against her school every now and again. Everyone on her team was always watching out for her, you know, on account of this family problem of hers that nobody wanted to talk about.

Something about her mother dying." She looked at me then, her eyes all sad, thinking about my mother. "Sorry," she said.

I shrugged. "It was a long time ago." Not that it stopped me from thinking about my mother. Not that it stopped me from missing her.

"I didn't know anything about Emily at first, except that she was on the other team and I wanted to win," Rebecca said. "So this one time I blocked her hard and she fell. Then she started crying. Crying! It was the league semi-finals. I wasn't trying to be mean or to hurt her. I was just trying to win." People think girls aren't as competitive as boys, that they don't play just as hard. But they do — at least, the athletic ones like Rebecca do. "She was crying and I said to her, Didn't your mother teach you to be a good sport? And all of a sudden she's crying even harder and running off the court and all the girls on her team are gathering around her. And then one of them comes up to me and tells me that I'm cruel. Cruel? I didn't even know Emily. How was I supposed to know about her mother? I'm still not sure what happened, except she died. After that, whenever our team went up against theirs, Emily would steer clear of me on the court." Rebecca shook her head. "They lost almost every game they played against us. Plus, the school she goes to now? My mom teaches there. She says Emily's dad is a real pain. He's one of those flashy rich guys, always with the manicure and the big diamond ring. He heads up the school fundraising committee. My mom says he acts like that entitles him to run the place."

Quick impression: Rebecca didn't think much of the Corwin family.

"I guess this means you don't think I should bother telling her about Mr. Henderson," I said.

Rebecca gave me a third, sharper look. "I don't have a lot of respect for Emily," she said. "Okay, I have none. At least, I didn't back in junior high. But if some old guy had gone through my stuff and had followed me to the subway, I'd appreciate knowing about it." She thought about what she had said and her expression changed.

"What?" I said.

"If a guy as cute as you told me that some old guy had been going through my stuff, I'd probably appreciate it a *lot*."

"Yeah? So?" I didn't know what she was getting at. But maybe that's because I was focusing on the first part of what she had said: Rebecca thought I was cute.

"You like me, don't you, Mike?"

"Yeah."

"So when you tell her, maybe I'd better be there. You know, so she doesn't get the wrong idea."

Oh. I smiled and then I kissed her again.

* * *

Sunday. The one day in the week when I could actually sleep in. The one day in the week when Riel lets me.

I got up around noon and went downstairs to find

something to eat. Riel was just coming up from the basement, carrying a basket full of fresh laundry. He was whistling. Nothing made him happier than clothes fresh from the dryer.

"I didn't hear you come in last night," I said.

"It was late." He passed me in the hall and continued up the stairs. "Your bed made?" he called over his shoulder.

"Not yet." I had just rolled out of it.

"So I'll leave your laundry outside your door, okay?"

Whatever. I went into the kitchen, wishing I could open the cupboard and find a box of cocoa puffs or maybe frosted flakes. But Riel didn't buy that kind of stuff. It's bad for you, he said the one time I asked him. So I settled for bread (seven-grain) with peanut butter (organic) and (yes!) the last of the strawberry jam Susan had given him last summer. I glanced through the Sunday paper while I ate.

"Hey," I said when Riel came into the kitchen with a pile of clean and folded dishtowels, "you know those bones they found? Well, they found the rest of the guy."

Riel grunted something. He was stacking the dishtowels in a drawer near the sink.

"It says it looks like the guy was shot. It says they can tell from the damage to a couple of the bones. It says they're looking for the bullet that did it," I said. "You know what that means, right?"

Riel looked at me and waited.

"It means I was right when I said the guy was murdered."

"Just because he was shot, that doesn't mean he was murdered," Riel said. "It could have been an accident."

"Sure. Some guy accidentally shoots some other guy and buries him in a shallow grave in the woods. That makes sense."

Riel shrugged. "Doesn't sound too likely, does it?" It was the closest he came to admitting I'd been right. "Hey, what did I hear about a fire at the community centre?"

"Some kid stole some cigarettes and was smoking them in the art room," I said. "And it was in the old part of the community centre where the sprinklers weren't working. Nobody was hurt, though." I got up to get some juice.

"Did you tell Teresa about your supervisor?"

"About the fire? She was there. I didn't have to tell — "

Riel shook his head. "You said you saw your supervisor — Mr. Henderson, right? — go into a girl's backpack. Did you tell Teresa about it?"

"Not yet."

He gave me a peeved look. "I thought we agreed that's what you would do."

"I forgot."

That earned me an even more peeved look. "When you say you're going to do something, you should do it."

"The thing is," I said, "I don't even know which

girl's backpack it was. There was a whole pile of them and he just looked in one. And he didn't take anything. *And* he saved that kid from the fire." I told Riel about that. I told him because I didn't want to have to tell him what *I* had done.

"Still," Riel said, "people have no business touching things that don't belong to them."

Neither did I. That was the problem.

"Mention it to her, will you, Mike?" Riel said.

"Okay."

"I mean it, Mike."

"*Okay.*"

CHAPTER FIVE

"Wow," I said.

"Your mouth is hanging open," Rebecca said.

She was right. I closed it. "Look at that one."

Rebecca grabbed my hand and lowered it. "Don't point. It's rude."

"But look at the size of that place," I said. "How many bathrooms you think they have in there?"

Rebecca shrugged. "Five," she said, "maybe six." Like it was no big deal.

We were on our way to Emily Corwin's school. To get there, we had to walk up a street that was lined on both sides with . . . mansions. It was the only word I could think of to describe the massive, beautiful houses, all of them on even more massive properties that were either fenced in or half-hidden behind stone walls, all of them with three- or four-car garages and little signs that warned that the place was protected by a security-alarm system. I'd never seen houses like these up close. I wasn't even sure I knew they existed.

"I bet some of them have swimming pools," I said.

"Probably," Rebecca said.

"I bet some of them have maids."

"Probably chauffeurs, too," Rebecca said. "You know what else some of them have?"

"What?"

"Stuck-up kids who think they're better than everyone else."

Oh.

"They're just houses, Mike. Houses that belong to people who have more money than they know what to do with."

Must be nice, I thought. But I didn't say it.

We turned a corner and Rebecca said, "There it is."

The school looked old, but well kept up. It was a big stone building set back from the street, surrounded by a rolling lawn. A high stone wall ran around it with an iron gate that Rebecca said they locked at night. It was open now, though, and on the other side of it, I saw girls. Girls hanging around the front of the school, talking. Girls over by the parking lot, one of them unlocking a candy-apple red Suzuki Tracker. Girls coming down the driveway, heading home to the big houses we had just passed. Rebecca marched up to the gate and then right through it. I caught her by the arm.

"You sure it's okay?" I said.

"They're just people, Mike. Just because they think they're special, doesn't mean you have to think so too."

"You don't like rich people, do you?"

"I don't like the ones I've met so far," she said. "Come on. You want to find her, don't you?"

Yeah, I did. But now that I was here, I didn't know where to start. There were so many girls, all of them with creamy rich-girl skin and thin rich-girl legs and shiny rich-girl hair — I don't why it is, but rich girls always have great-looking hair —

and Mountain Equipment Co-op backpacks over coats and jackets that looked expensive. All those rich girls either ignored me or looked at me like, Who did I think I was? Like I didn't belong. Or maybe I just imagined that.

"She's probably gone home already," I said.

"Let's find out." Rebecca stepped in front of two girls who were walking toward us. "Excuse me. I'm looking for Emily Corwin. Do you know if she's still around?"

The way the girls looked at Rebecca, it was obvious they knew that she didn't belong here either. But one of them said, "Yeah. I think she's in the music room."

"Thanks," Rebecca said, her voice cool. Thanks, as in, *Thanks for condescending to talk to me.* Or maybe I imagined that, too.

Rebecca walked up to the front door and yanked it open.

"You sure we can go in?" I said.

Rebecca shook her head again. "Get a grip, Mike. My mother works here, remember? I've been here a million times."

She smiled and said hi to a grey-haired old guy in a little office just inside the front door.

"That's Lawrence," she said. "He's the porter."

"Porter?"

"The guy who watches the door, makes sure no one comes in who shouldn't."

I glanced back at Lawrence. He looked like he was well past mandatory retirement age.

"What does he do, wrestle trespassers to the ground?"

"He's got a button under his desk," Rebecca said. "He presses it."

She led me up some stairs, down one hallway and then along another. Through a door to another hallway, I saw guys in hard hats. I wondered what was going on. Rebecca glanced through the window.

"They're renovating the pool," she said. "Making it bigger. In the meantime, the swim team has to practise at *our* community centre."

Our community centre?

"You really know your way around here," I said.

She shrugged and pulled open a door. I saw a girl inside with long blond hair. She was fastening the clasps on a small instrument case. It looked like maybe a clarinet case. The girl was definitely Emily. While she was putting her instrument away, she was talking to a guy who was in the room with her. She was saying, "If you don't go now, Neil, I'll scream. If I scream, teachers will come running. They won't just throw you out, either, Neil, because I'll tell them you were harassing me. I'll see to it that they call the cops. You've got to the count of five. One . . . two . . . "

Rebecca looked at me, one of her pale eyebrows arched a little higher than the other one. At the time, I didn't see her point. For all I knew, the guy *had* been harassing poor Emily. In retrospect, I should have known better.

Rebecca cleared her throat. Emily looked over at

us. Neil kept looking at Emily. Poor guy — if you ask me, he had it bad.

Emily smiled at me. Then she looked at Neil and said, "Three . . . "

Neil straightened up, like he felt he had to prove to us that he wasn't being pushed around. He said, "Sarah was never anything like you." Then he turned and looked hard at me, but not so hard at Rebecca. He left the room. Emily didn't even watch him go.

"Hi," she said to me.

"Hi," I said. "I would have called you, but you're not in the phone book."

Her eyes kind of sparkled when I said that, and she smiled again, very sweetly.

"We're unlisted," she said. "My dad doesn't like to be bothered at home by people we don't know. You know, like telemarketers."

Beside me, Rebecca made a disapproving noise, the kind you associate with someone rolling her eyes. Rich people, she was probably thinking, they don't like to be disturbed like the rest of us.

Emily looked directly at her, making it clear she knew what was going on. "You still playing aggressive basketball?" she said.

"No," Rebecca said. I waited for her to say something like, You still crying every time someone blocks you? But she didn't. Instead she said, "Mike wants to tell you something."

"Oh?" Emily turned to me again, and again her face relaxed.

I guess I hadn't expected that we would actually find her, because I hadn't thought through what I was going to say. She looked at me, waiting.

"Mr. Henderson seems to be interested in you," I said finally. "*Really* interested, if you know what I mean."

"No," she said, "I don't know what you mean. Who is Mr. Henderson?"

"The janitor," I said. "At the community centre."

"The community centre? You mean, where I met you?" She gave Rebecca a little smile.

I nodded.

"What do you mean, he's *really* interested in me?"

"I saw him watching you."

"You mean, like you were watching me that time?"

I felt Rebecca's eyes on me.

"Mr. Henderson is an old guy," I said. "I saw him going through your wallet."

Emily stood there, a hand on her hip, half-smiling, half-suspicious. "I caught *you* going through my wallet."

"Because I wanted to see what he was doing," I said. "And I saw him follow you to the subway."

She was still smiling, but now she also seemed annoyed. I could see it in her eyes. "You're kidding, right?" she said. "This is some kind of joke, right? Did Becky the Basher here put you up to this?"

Becky the Basher?

"It's Rebecca," Rebecca said. "And I've never been fouled for *bashing*."

"It's no joke," I said. I couldn't believe Emily's reaction. "I'm telling you, Mr. Henderson was watching you. He followed you. He went through your stuff. I thought you should know."

She studied me a moment. Then she said, "Well, thanks for telling me." She didn't sound even remotely grateful. "We're not going to swim there again for a while. Our coach finally arranged practice time at a place closer to here. So I guess this Mr. — what did you say his name was?"

"Henderson."

"Mr. Henderson is going to have to ogle someone else." She picked up the instrument case. She looked at me and then at Rebecca. Then she set the case down again, fished a pen out of her pocket and looked around for some paper. Finally she grabbed a piece of sheet music from a rack and scribbled something on it. "My phone number," she said. "My cell. You know, in case someone else takes an interest in me that you think I should know about." She handed it to me, then she said, "What about you?"

"Me?"

"Your phone number," she said. "Can I have it?"

I recited it and she wrote it on another sheet of music. Mr. Korchak at my school would have flipped out if anyone scribbled on school music. I guess private schools were different. Or rich kids were.

"Well then," she said, "I guess I'd better run." She flashed a great big grin at Rebecca as she strolled out of the music room, her narrow hips swaying and making me remember how great she had looked in her navy blue Speedo.

"A-hem!" Rebecca said.

I turned to face her. "Becky the Basher?" I said.

"Personally," Rebecca said, "if it was me, I'd tell creepy Mr. Henderson where to find her. I'd even draw him a map."

"It was your idea to tell her."

"I guess I was hoping she'd changed. She hasn't." She thought for a moment. "No, wait a minute, she has. She's gotten worse."

"She's turned into one of those stuck-up rich kids you don't like, right?"

"The way she acts, she could be the original blue-print. You know what I think? I think she uses that thing about her mother. I think she plays on the sympathy. You keeping that?"

"Huh?"

She was looking at the piece of sheet music in my hand, the one that Emily had scrawled her phone number on.

"Uh, no," I said. I tossed it into the wastepaper basket near the door.

"So," Rebecca said, smiling now, "you want to meet my mom?"

"Sure."

"Follow me." She led the way out of the room. As I passed the wastepaper basket, I scooped out the crumpled sheet of paper and jammed it into my pocket. I don't think Rebecca noticed. I wasn't so sure about Neil, though. He was in the hall just outside the door. I saw him when I straightened up. He didn't say anything. He just looked at me. I ran to catch up with Rebecca.

* * *

Riel was sitting at the dining room table marking test papers when I got home from the community centre that night. He glanced up.

"Did you talk to Teresa?"

"Yeah." I really had talked to her. I had done it because I knew Riel would ask me. He'd probably check too. I had told her that I wasn't sure I should say anything, I wasn't even sure if I had seen it right, but I had noticed Mr. Henderson holding a girl's backpack and it was open and I just thought I should say something, you know, in case anything had fallen out or gone missing. She had frowned and asked if I thought he had taken anything. I said no, I was pretty sure he hadn't, but that I had been there and I didn't want anyone to think that I had taken anything, you know, in case anyone reported anything missing. She gave me another look, like she was trying to figure out what was going on, but she said, no, nothing had been reported missing. She thanked me for telling her, but I could see she wasn't exactly sure what to do with the information.

"And?" Riel said.

"And she said it was good I mentioned it."

Riel's smile was one hundred percent I-told-you-so. "There's a message for you," he said. "A girl called."

"Rebecca?"

"Emily. She said you had her number. She wants you to call her back." He looked at me. "I don't remember you mentioning an Emily before. Is she from school?"

"She's from the community centre," I said. I was thinking, Emily called? Why? What did she want? "Is it okay if I take the phone upstairs?" The phone in the kitchen was a cordless.

He nodded. "Just put it back when you're finished."

I got the phone and took it up to my room. I closed the door, fished out the crumpled piece of paper I had shoved into my jeans pocket, and smoothed it out with the back of my hand. She answered on the second ring.

"It's me," I said. "Mike?" Like it was a question, like I wasn't sure who I was. I don't know why she made me so nervous, but she did. Way more nervous than I'd ever been around Rebecca, or even Jen.

"Hi, McGill," she said, sounding cool, calling me by my last name. "I was wondering — do you think you could come over to my place tomorrow after school? I need to talk to you about something."

The correct answer was no. No way. Rebecca would never speak to me again if I said yes to Emily Corwin. And I cared about Rebecca — a lot.

"Yes or no, McGill?" she said.

I can't explain why, but instead of giving the correct answer, I heard myself say, "Yeah, I guess."

"It's a request," she said, "not an order." She sounded amused. I imagined her smiling. "You don't have to if you don't want to."

"No, I do," I said. Maybe I said it a little too fast. I heard her laugh. "It's just — I don't know where you live."

"You have a pencil?"

"Yeah," I said, while I scrabbled for one in my desk drawer. I wrote down the street and the number of her house and jotted down her instructions.

"Great," she said. "And McGill? Just you, okay? Leave Becky at home. Okay?"

"Okay," I said. That's when I heard it in my voice — eagerness. I wanted to see her again. I shouldn't have, but I did. I wanted to talk to her, maybe get to know her a little better. I wanted to go to her house and see what that looked like too. Maybe Rebecca didn't like her — maybe she didn't like any rich people — but I didn't feel the same way. I was curious — about her, about where she lived, about what kind of life she lived. That didn't mean I wanted to go out with her. I was happy with Rebecca. But a guy can want to expand his horizons, right? A guy can talk to one girl, even drop by her house, while he's seeing another girl, right? It's not a crime, is it? It's just one visit, to a big house, a rich girl's house. And, no problem, I wouldn't bring Rebecca. Heck, I wouldn't even *tell* Rebecca. As I hung up the phone, I wondered why Emily wanted to see me. I wondered if she felt the same way I did. I wondered if she wanted to get to know me too.

CHAPTER SIX

The woman who opened the door for me at Emily's house looked about sixty. She told me to wait while she let Emily know I was there.

"Is that your grandmother?" I said when Emily finally appeared.

For a moment Emily looked confused. Then she said, "Oh. You mean Estelle. She's our housekeeper. Why?"

"Just wondering," I said. I had never met anyone who had a housekeeper. Jen's parents were pretty well off. They lived in a big house in a really nice neighbourhood and drove his and hers Beamers. They had a cleaning lady who came in three times a week. Whenever they had a party, they hired a bartender and a couple of people to pass out the hors d'oeuvres and to clean up afterwards. But they didn't have a housekeeper. And, it turns out, at least in comparison to Emily, they weren't rich.

Emily lived on a tree-lined street not far from her school. To get from the street to her house, you had to press a button at a big black iron gate set into the high stone wall that enclosed the property. Then you had to wait for someone — in this case, Estelle the housekeeper — to ask you over the intercom who you were and what you wanted. Then you had to wait for her to check with someone inside the house — Emily, I guess — before she pressed the button inside the house that unlocked the gate.

The house itself was set way back from the street. I followed a stone path to the front door and was about to press the bell when the door flew open. Emily grinned out at me.

"You surprised me, McGill," she said. She seemed to like calling me by my last name. "You're right on time."

I didn't know why she was so surprised by that.

"Come on in," she said.

I stepped into the kind of front hall that I had only ever seen before on TV or in the movies. It was big, with a round table in the middle of it and a vase of fresh flowers in the middle of the table. The floor, which was made of some kind of tile, was so clean it sparkled. A curving staircase led to the second floor. Through a door to one side of the stairs was the living room — I found out later that it was the *formal* living room and that there was another, less formal, one at the back of the house that overlooked what Emily called the gardens. To the other side of the stairs was the dining room. I must have been gaping at all the art on the walls, not to mention the furniture that had definitely not come from IKEA or Sears, because Emily said, "Yeah, I know. It's like living in a museum. Touch anything and my dad goes nuts. He's got every item in the house catalogued, photographed and identified. And I am not kidding. He's very big on his stuff, my dad is." It sounded to me like she didn't share his enthusiasm. She called to Estelle that we were going upstairs. Then she said, "Come on, McGill."

"Where are we going?"

"My room," she said. "Where else?"

Her room? Jen's parents never let me go into Jen's room. Of course, after the first couple of times I'd gone over there, Jen's parents wouldn't even let me in the house. I felt more welcome at Rebecca's house, but we always hung out in the solarium or in the family room, never in Rebecca's room.

"Are you coming or what?" Emily said.

I glanced around. It didn't look like anyone was going to stop me, so I followed her up the stairs.

The upstairs hall had more furniture in it than Riel had in his whole house. There was a sofa, two armchairs and a table in front of a huge round window at the front of the house. Halfway down the hall was another table with more fresh flowers on it and a chair beside it, so if you got tired walking around in all that space you could sit down and have a rest. A bookshelf at the far end of the hall ran all the way up to the ceiling. It had a ladder attached to it so that you could climb up and reach the books at the top.

"Looks great, doesn't it?" Emily said. "I don't think my father has even read half of them. In fact, I'd be surprised if he's read any of them."

She led me through a door to the left of the bookcase.

I blinked when I stepped inside.

"This is your bedroom?" I said. It was huge — you

could fit four, maybe six of my rooms in there.

She looked at me as if I had just emerged from a spaceship.

"Bed," she said, pointing to a four-poster bed that had light blue curtains hanging around it. "Room," she said, twirling like a dancer and pointing at the four walls. "Bedroom."

Besides the bed that looked like it belonged to a princess who maybe lived in a palace, she also had a sofa, a table in front of the sofa, two big armchairs, an entertainment centre that included a stereo, CD player, a pair of those really small but really powerful and high-quality speakers, TV, VCR and DVD player, a desk, a computer, a couple of floor-to-ceiling bookcases of her own — and the ceilings were high — and her own bathroom, which, I could see through the open door, had a whirlpool bath in it.

"Nice," I said.

"Be it ever so humble."

Right. I looked around some more. There were a couple of pictures sitting on a table that was covered with make-up stuff. One was a nice-looking middle-aged guy, heavily tanned, great haircut, sharp suit, hands crossed in front of him.

"Your dad?" I said.

"Yeah. Mister Glitz."

"Huh?"

"See that ring?" she said. I looked closer at the picture. "Diamond." A huge diamond. It sparkled on the third finger of his left — no, his right — hand.

"You wouldn't believe how many carats," she said. "The cufflinks too."

Cufflinks? Who wore cufflinks? I looked again.

"Diamonds," she said. "And check his right ear." I looked a third time. "Diamond stud." Yup, there it was. Pretty big for a stud, if you ask me. "He thinks it's cool," Emily said. "I tell him, a guy his age, that's not cool, that's pathetic. But he loves diamonds. Loves the sparkle. So I call him Mister Glitz, you know, to get under his skin."

"They must be worth a lot," I said.

"You bet. And he's got them all catalogued, marked — in this case, printed — and insured to the max. Like I said, everything in this house is identified, catalogued and insured."

"Printed?"

"You know, like fingerprinted."

I looked at the rock on his finger again. "How do you take a fingerprint of a diamond?" I said. "Aren't they all pretty much alike?"

"No, McGill, they are not," she said. "If I've learned anything living with my dad, it's that diamonds are *not* all alike." What did she mean, living with her dad? She made it sound like she hadn't always lived with him. "And because they're not all alike, you can take fingerprints of them. Well, sort of. You can take what they call a gemprint. The idea is the same as a fingerprint. It's a laser scan of the diamond. Jewellers — *good* jewellers — call it the DNA of diamonds."

The things I didn't know. I looked at the second

photo. Emily's dad again — except he wasn't wearing the huge rock on his finger in this one — a woman and two little girls. One looked like Emily when she was maybe four or five. The other girl looked older.

"Your mom?" I said, pointing at the woman.

She nodded.

"And, what, your sister?" She nodded again and I looked back at the picture. "She looks like your dad. You look more like your mom. Is she at university now?"

"Who?"

"Your sister." Geeze, who did she think I meant? "She's older than you, so I thought maybe she was away at university."

"No," Emily said, "she isn't."

I waited for her to say more, but she didn't. Maybe she and her sister didn't get along. Maybe they even hated each other.

Emily perched on the edge of her bed. "Have a seat, McGill."

I sank down onto one of the armchairs.

"So," she said, "what'd you have to do to end up at the community centre?"

"Huh?"

"You're there on a community service order, right? What'd you do?"

"How do you know that?" I said. Teresa Rego knew why I was there because she was the director of the community centre. Maybe Mr. Henderson knew too, maybe they had told him. But it wasn't supposed to be common knowledge.

"I heard someone mention it, you know, like a rumour." She smiled at me again, looking all innocent. "Which you just confirmed." When I didn't say anything right away, she said, "It doesn't bother me that you've been in trouble with the police, if that's what you're worried about. If it bothered me, I wouldn't have invited you over."

"I'm not worried," I said. "I don't care." It wasn't one hundred percent true, but what was I supposed to do? Whine about it?

"So? What'd you do?" Her eyes had a gleam to them. Maybe she was one of those girls who got off on tough guys. Maybe I was the closest she had ever come to a real criminal. Maybe she liked that. I wasn't sure how I felt about it though. "Come on, McGill, you can tell me."

"I stole something."

"Money?"

"Geeze, no."

She seemed disappointed. "What, then? Jewellery?" She looked closely at me and shook her head. "CDs? Oh, I know." Her eyes flashed. "Stereo equipment!"

"I'd rather not say," I said, mainly because what I had stolen was a box of cupcakes off the back of a bakery truck. I had the feeling that wasn't what she wanted to hear.

She shrugged. "I also heard about your uncle," she said. "Is it true?"

"Is what true?"

"What he did." She recited a bunch of facts about what had happened to Billy.

"Where'd you hear that?" I said. I couldn't imagine a bunch of rich girls sitting around talking about my uncle.

She just shrugged again. "So, is it true?"

She didn't have the whole story, but she hadn't said anything that wasn't true, either, so I said, "Yeah."

"Cool," she said.

"Cool?" She was cute — no, make that beautiful. Up close, she was as pretty as any model in any fashion magazine. But she was also kind of weird. "You said you needed to talk to me about something."

"Right." She pulled her legs up onto the bed and sat there cross-legged. "I was thinking about that guy you said was interested in me. Mr. Henderson? I was thinking I'd like to know more about him."

"Yeah?"

"You know, since he's so interested in me and since he went through my stuff, I thought maybe you should find out more about him for me. I'd like to know what kind of a guy would do something like that."

She thought *I* should find out more about him? "Why don't you just call the police?"

"And tell them what?"

"That you caught him going through your stuff."

"But I didn't. I caught *you* going through my stuff."

I looked at her.

"I guess I could tell them that," she said. "And I guess since you're at the community centre on a community service order, they'd probably have to tell the director of the community centre. And then — how does it work?" She looked at me, like she was trying to figure it out, like she didn't already know exactly what would happen. "She'd have to tell your probation officer or whatever it's called, wouldn't she?"

"It's called youth worker," I said.

"Right," she said, nodding. "She'd have to tell your youth worker. And I'm just guessing, but I bet the news wouldn't go down too well, huh? A guy doing a community service order because he's a thief and he's found stealing a hundred dollars out of a girl's wallet."

"Hey!" I said. I stood up fast. What was going on here? "I never stole anything from you."

"Gosh," she said, "then how come I had a hundred dollars in my wallet before I saw you go into it and it was all gone after you ran away?"

Now she was confusing me. "I *didn't* run away."

"Did I mention that my dad has a lot of lawyer friends? A lot of Crown attorney friends too." She reached over, opened a drawer in her bedside table and pulled out something in a Ziploc baggie. A shiny black wallet. *Her* wallet. What was it doing in a plastic baggie?

"Right after I caught you," she said, "I put it in here so that nothing would get smudged. You know what I mean, McGill?"

Geeze. I knew exactly what she meant. What was with her?

"You were fingerprinted, right?" she said. "When they arrest you for stealing, they fingerprint you. Right?"

"What are you doing? Blackmailing me?" Why would she even bother? "You don't even know me."

"You shouldn't touch other people's stuff, McGill. It can get you in trouble. You're lucky I decided to check you out before I reported you."

I had to remind myself that she was my age because, boy, she acted like someone a whole lot older. And a whole lot more calculating.

"That's it. I'm outta here."

"With my diamond earrings?" she said. She dangled something from one hand — something that glinted.

"Geeze, no," I said. What was happening?

"Come on, McGill." She flashed a sweet smile. "I'm not asking you to do anything you haven't done maybe a hundred times before. I just want you to check out the guy for me. I want to know who he is and what he wants with me. Then I want to find a way to teach him a lesson. You want to help me, don't you?" When I didn't answer, she said, "If you don't want to help me, the least you could do is help yourself. I'll give you the wallet when it's over. You can wipe it clean yourself. You can burn it if you want to, I don't care."

"You're not what I thought," I said.

"Yeah, well, I thought you'd be different too. I

thought you wouldn't be such a wuss." She dangled her diamond earrings again. "What do you say?"

* * *

I passed through the gate and heard it click shut behind me. I turned to look back at the house — enormous, sturdy, the windows gleaming as if they'd all just been washed, the whole place filled with expensive stuff, the kind of stuff I wished I had — well, some of it. And inside, Emily, who had everything and, you know what, who didn't seem all that much happier than me. Who was pretty and rich and just like Rebecca said — not nice. Emily seemed to be enjoying having me in a spot, maybe even more than she enjoyed all that stuff she had.

I turned again to take the long walk to the closest bus stop and that's when I saw him on the sidewalk on the other side of the street. Neil. I looked at him. He looked right back at me. I kept walking.

A car was cruising up the street. Boy, a really cool car. A Jaguar. Vintage. It was a colour they call midnight blue. Tinted windows. Low, sleek, silent. A rich man's car. It slid up the street, heading home to some mansion or other. The guy in it had probably made a million dollars today alone. He was probably going home and was going to have his maid or his housekeeper or his wife make him a martini so he could celebrate. That's what Jen's dad used to do when he signed some big-deal lawyer contract, he'd kick back and have a few martinis and tell Jen and her mother all about it.

Jen used to say it was like listening to a golf tournament on the radio, it was that boring.

This Jag, though, it was purring along one minute and then was stopped right there in the middle of the street the next. I couldn't see the driver, but I saw Neil looking at the car and I heard a man's voice yelling something. Neil stared at the car, maybe at the driver, who must have put down the passenger-side window, otherwise how could he be yelling at Neil? Neil said something I couldn't hear, I only saw his mouth move. Whatever he said, it got a reaction. The driver's side door opened and a man got out — *jumped* out. A big man in a leather jacket. He moved fast around the front of the car. Neil seemed to freeze when he saw him. By the time Neil decided maybe he should get out of there, the man had grabbed him and was shaking him hard. It looked like the kind of shaking that could rattle your teeth and maybe even give you whiplash. And, boy, the man was like a giant compared to Neil.

Neil looked around — there was no one else on the street, no cars, no people, nothing. Just the Jaguar sitting there and the big man shaking him and Neil saying, "Hey, hey!" like that was all he could get out.

I ran across the street and grabbed the man by the arm. Underneath the leather jacket he felt like he was made of steel. There was no way I was going to make this guy let go, not by force anyway.

"Hey, mister," I said. "Hey, you better leave

him alone. Someone called the cops."

The guy shook Neil harder and told him, "Stay away from here, you understand me? Stay away."

"Mister." I pulled on his arm again. "The lady across the street, she ran in to call the cops."

The man seemed to look right through me at first. Then his eyes cleared. He focused in on me and finally nodded. He let go of Neil.

"Go on," I said to Neil. "You better get out of here."

Neil stared at me too. It was weird. These two guys, staring at me like they were both in some kind of dream. Then Neil turned and ran down the street, and the man got back into his Jag. I watched him drive a couple of metres up the street and then make a left into Emily's driveway.

* * *

I headed down the street. Neil was standing a couple of blocks away, his hands in his jacket pockets, face hard and serious. He watched me walk toward him. I would have been willing to bet he was waiting for me. I could have crossed the street to avoid him, but what was the point? If he wanted to say something to me, he'd say it one way or the other.

What he said was, "What are you? The new boyfriend?" He said it like he'd already decided I was and he didn't like me because of it.

"What're you?" I said. "The *old* boyfriend?" Under his jacket he was wearing a uniform top and a nametag with the Blockbuster logo on it. The guy worked at Blockbuster, which meant he was not in Emily's league.

He kept glaring at me, but he didn't scare me. He hadn't put up any fight at all against the guy in the Jag, so how tough could he be?

He looked me over, checked out my parka and my jeans and my sneakers. Then he said, "Well, good luck if you are, because Jim will never let you make a move."

"Jim?"

"Emily's father. The guy in the Jag. He's not gonna let you get near her."

It had all happened so fast, but now I remembered the photo in Emily's room. James Corwin looked a whole lot bigger in real life.

"He's not gonna let you near her," Neil said again.

"Yeah, well, I'm not sure I want to get near her."

He looked at me again like he was mad all over again, only this time it was because now I *wasn't* interested in Emily.

"She comes across a little messed up sometimes," he said, "but she's not bad."

"Really?" If he wanted to believe that, he could be my guest.

"It's her dad. He's one of those guys who really marks his territory, you know what I mean?"

I didn't.

"He's possessive," Neil said. "Big time. That's how come he's divorced. Emily's mother couldn't stand it. And with Emily, well, no one's good enough for his little girl."

"Been there," I said, because I knew exactly what he meant. Jen's dad had felt exactly the same way about Jen — at least, he had when I was seeing her. "Look, I'm not interested in her. And I already have a girlfriend. The girl I was with at Emily's school the other day."

"The redhead?"

I nodded.

He relaxed a little. "Thanks for getting him off me," he said.

I told him it was no big deal.

"Emily really isn't bad," he said, "if you actually know her."

"And you do?" I said.

"Since second grade," he said. Then, "I have to get to work." He jerked his head left and I saw a Blockbuster on the corner.

I told him good luck because, boy, if he had his heart set on Emily, he was going to need a lot of it. Then, because I was wondering, I said, "Do you get free rentals?"

* * *

By the time I got home, I was starving. I made a sandwich, flipped on the little TV in the kitchen, and sat down at the kitchen table to eat. I caught a news flash during one of the advertising breaks — the police had located a bullet "in the vicinity" of the bones they had found in the woods. According to the announcer, the police "believed" the bullet "could be" associated with the bones found earlier. Details at eleven.

CHAPTER SEVEN

I couldn't tell Rebecca about what had happened. She would be mad that I'd gone to Emily's house in the first place. She'd also be mad that I hadn't told her. She'd probably think it was because I was interested in Emily — which maybe I had been a little, at first. But after talking to her, after listening to what she had to say, all I wanted to do was stay away from her forever. Except that now it wasn't safe to do that either.

I guess I could have talked to Riel about it, but I could just imagine how that would play out.

Me: There's this girl, she's threatening to call the cops on me and tell them I stole a hundred dollars from her wallet.

Riel: You stole a hundred dollars from a girl's wallet?

Me: No. She just caught me going through her wallet.

Riel: You went through her wallet?

Me: I didn't take anything.

Riel: But you went through her wallet?

Me: I just wanted to see who she was. I didn't take anything.

Riel: You went through a girl's wallet without her permission?

Yeah, that would be productive.

So I told the only person I could think of.

"Am I ever glad I didn't let you set me up with

her," Sal said when I finished the story.

"What am I going to do?"

"You think she's serious?"

I pictured Emily sitting cross-legged on her bed, dangling the Ziploc baggie containing her shiny black wallet with my fingerprints all over it. "Yeah," I said. "She looks all sweet and innocent, you know? But she isn't. She's . . . weird. Like this is some big kick. Some kind of power trip. And you know what else? She knew about Billy."

"I bet she's a killer in the pool," Sal said. "She sounds like she plays to win or she doesn't play at all." He gave me a sympathetic look. "Now what?"

"Now I guess I do what she wants — that way I get the wallet and get it over with."

"You know how you're going to do it?"

I'd given it some thought. "Check out his locker first, I guess. See what I can find out about him and take it from there."

If I'd been talking to my (used-to-be) best friend Vin — *if* Vin were still around — I wouldn't even have had to ask. Vin would have offered to help. He probably would have come up with a plan for how to do it. And Vin would have been begging to meet Emily. For Vin, the badder and weirder, the better. But Vin wasn't around and wouldn't be for a while.

Sal wasn't anything like Vin. Especially now, with his dad not doing too well, with his job, with the idea he had now that he was going to go to university, he was going to get an education, he was going to make something of himself — that's the way he put it. So Sal played it safe. He followed all the rules. He did all his work. He kept his head down. It was like he was following John Riel's Book of Rules, chapter by chapter, line by line.

So I was surprised when he said, "Sounds like you're going to need some help. Sounds like you need a lookout."

At first I thought he was going to suggest someone. But he didn't. Then I got it.

"*You?*" I said. I guess I sounded more surprised than I should have.

"Thanks, Sal," Sal said. "I knew I could count on you, Sal," Sal said. "You're a real friend, Sal," he said. He looked at me and shook his head.

* * *

Riel had to attend some kind of teacher meeting after school. He didn't get home before I left for work, which was good. If he had seen me, he might have noticed how nervous I was. Boy, was I jumpy. Maybe Emily had some idea that I was a thief, that taking things and breaking into places was second nature to me. But it wasn't. What she was asking me to do — okay, *telling* me — wasn't something that I did every day of the week. Or ever. Still, I had a plan.

Step one: The key. Every Wednesday night, a group of what Mr. Henderson called mobility-impaired teens came to the community centre for a special swim class. Some of them also had other disabilities. All of them needed special help to get out of their wheelchairs and into the pool. Mr.

Henderson always stayed in the pool area the whole time they were there, helping the two instructors and the volunteers get the kids into the pool, helping them if they needed to get out again for any reason during the class, which sometimes they did, and then helping them all get out again at the end. Mr. Henderson always wore a T-shirt and bathing suit when he helped out, a baggy pair of old trunks that looked like old-geezer Bermuda shorts.

I waited until he was busy with one of the kids. Then I walked out onto the deck.

"Mr. Henderson?"

He didn't hear me at first. The kid he was with was big — taller than me, and heavier too. Mr. Henderson and another guy who looked like maybe he was a university student were carrying the kid down the steps in the shallow end, one of them on either side of the kid. I waited until they had lowered him into the water.

"Mr. Henderson?"

He turned and scowled at me. One thing I had learned: Mr. Henderson was a guy who didn't like to be disturbed.

"I'm sorry," I said, "I know you're busy. But I got locked out of the utility room on the third floor."

"How'd you manage that?" he said. He sounded annoyed.

I shrugged and tried to look apologetic. "I had it propped open," I said. The utility room doors were on a big spring. They closed and locked automatically unless you propped them open or wedged something in between the door and the jamb to keep them open. "I don't know. I must have banged into it."

Mr. Henderson looked at the big kid who was floating on his back in the pool now. Then he looked back at me.

"I guess I could do something else," I said. "You know, until you're finished here."

He looked at the clock on the wall behind the diving board, then at me, then over at the door to the men's change room, and then back at me. I had the feeling that if it were up to him, I'd be fired. Immediately. For stupidity.

"I'm sorry," I said again.

The university student said something to Mr. Henderson, but I couldn't hear what it was. Mr. Henderson held up his hand in a "just a minute" gesture.

"My overalls are hanging on a hook in there," he said to me, nodding in the direction of the change room. "My keys are in the pocket. Unlock the door, wedge it open again — securely this time — and then put the keys back. You think you can do that?"

I nodded. "I'm sorry," I said for the third time. Three's the charm, right?

He looked at me for another moment before turning back to the kid who was floating in the water.

I went into the change room, found Mr. Henderson's overalls, pulled out the key chain and unhooked it from the belt loop it was fastened to.

There were a couple of dozen keys on the ring, all colour-coded. I knew from watching Mr. Henderson that the yellow dots were for utility closets, the red dots for activity rooms, the green for offices, and the blue for the pool area. That left a grand total of three other keys that didn't have coloured dots on them. How hard could it be to find the one I was looking for?

I took the keys down to the basement where Sal was waiting for me.

One look at Sal told me that he would never make a good thief. He didn't have the right instincts. For example, when he showed up at the community centre to help me, he was wearing his uniform from McDonald's, including his name badge that said, Hi, I'm Sal. I stared at it.

"Don't you want to at least put that in your pocket?" I said. "You know, be anonymous if you can't be inconspicuous?"

He glanced down at the badge but didn't unpin it. "The way I figure it," he said, "the uniform clears me. I mean, who'd believe a guy would show up to basically do something illegal while he's wearing a uniform and a name badge?"

Maybe I was wrong about Sal. There was a certain crazy, devious logic to what he said. I positioned him by the stairs. Actually, there were two sets of stairs that led into the basement — one at either side of the building. But from where Sal was standing, at the bottom of one set, you could see the door at the bottom of the other set.

"Take out your math book," I said. Sal always took his backpack to work with him because he always had a couple of breaks during the evening when he could get some homework done.

"Why math?" he said.

"It's the heaviest book we have." It was big and thick and weighed as much as a paving stone. "You hang out here, pretend you're studying, and if you see anyone — anyone at all — drop the book. Drop it flat and it'll make a big bang. I'll hear it."

"Then what?"

"Then I duck into the boiler room until whoever it is leaves." Assuming I could make it into the boiler room in time. "Then I go up to the change room and replace the keys." Assuming I had the chance, assuming the person who prompted Sal to drop his math book wasn't Mr. Henderson, out of the pool for some reason and looking for me — and his keys.

Now for step two: the break-in.

I tried the first non-colour-coded key. It didn't turn. Neither did the second one. Key number three did the trick, though. I looked all around, even though Sal was standing near the stairs, and pressed my ear to the door before I turned the knob.

The maintenance room was small and square, and contained a four-unit bank of lockers, an apartment-size fridge, and a sink with a narrow counter on either side of it on which sat a coffee maker, a small microwave oven and a radio. Four lockers, but Mr. Henderson was the only maintenance person on staff and, as far as I had been able to figure out, the only person who had a key to the cubby-hole of a room — which was probably why none of the lockers had locks on them.

I closed the door behind me and crossed to the lockers. Mr. Henderson used the one on the far right, closest to the sink. I had seen him hang his jacket in it. I opened it.

And was disappointed.

On the top shelf: the toque he wore when he worked outside shovelling snow or grooming the rink. Hanging on one hook: a ratty old sweater he sometimes wore. I checked the pockets — nothing. On the other hook: his parka. I dug into the pockets. Nothing — well, nothing except some crumpled up (and, I hoped, unused) tissues. On the floor of the locker: the work boots he wore when he was outside.

I checked the other three lockers. They were all empty. I checked the fridge. Apart from an apple and a container of yoghurt, it was empty. I checked the drawer next to the sink — it contained a can opener, some cutlery, a handful of paper napkins and some little packages of ketchup, mustard, salt and pepper. I checked the cupboard under the sink. Nothing there except a sponge, a bottle of cleaner and a garbage can. I started to close the cupboard door — then stopped, reached in and pulled out the garbage can. I held my breath when I opened the lid. But the only thing inside was a crumpled up plastic bag from a drugstore. I pulled it out and was looking inside when . . .

83

Blam!

Geeze.

I shoved the drugstore bag into my pocket, jammed the garbage can back under the sink, and ducked out of the room, pulling the door shut behind me and then fumbling with the keys, trying to get the right one, trying to lock the door again because, unlike the utility closet doors, this one didn't lock automatically. My heart pounded. My hands shook so badly that I dropped the keys. Sal wouldn't make a good thief? *I* wouldn't make a good thief. If Riel had been here, and if he had looked at it the right way, he would have been relieved.

"Psst!"

I froze for a second. Then, like it was someone else who was making it happen, my head turned and I saw Sal standing out in the hall, away from the stairs, looking mostly embarrassed.

"I dropped it by accident," he said, keeping his voice low. "Sorry."

Geeze.

I hurried down the hall toward him. "It's okay," I said. The truth was, I was relieved it was over. Well, mostly over.

"Did you find anything?" he said.

I shook my head. I had found exactly nothing that would tell me — or Emily — anything more about Mr. Henderson than I already knew, which was just about nothing. Sal looked disappointed.

"I better get these keys back," I said.

Sal said he'd better get to work. And that was that. I went back upstairs, slipped the keys back into Mr. Henderson's pocket, and climbed the stairs to the third floor to finish my mopping. By the time I was ready to move down to the second floor, Mr. Henderson was there with his keys to open the second-floor utility room door for me. His hair was still wet from the pool.

When I went downstairs at the end of my shift, Riel was standing inside the main doors. My first thought: something bad has happened. Maybe Emily had called the house again. Maybe this time she said something to Riel. But when he came toward me, he didn't look worried or mad or disappointed — nothing like that.

Still, to be on the safe side, I said, "Is something wrong?"

"Yeah, something's wrong," he said, which gave me a sinking feeling. What now, I wondered. "I was just talking to Teresa." She was a friend of Riel's. For a quiet, serious guy, he knew a lot of people. He put one hand on my shoulder and shook his head. I swallowed hard, thinking she must have said something bad about me. But what? I hadn't done anything wrong. Well, unless you counted the keys I had just stolen, the snooping I had just done, and that thing with Emily's wallet. I was glad I had talked to Teresa about Mr. Henderson. Riel had probably mentioned that to her. Oh-oh. Maybe Emily had double-crossed me. Maybe *she'd* spoken to Teresa.

"Boy, does she ever put in long hours," Riel said. "Anyway, she said you're doing great — always on time, always polite, no complaints from the guy you're working with."

"Yeah, well . . . " I shrugged.

"That's not why I'm here, though."

Right. He was here because something was wrong. I waited.

"The way I figure it," Riel said, "between school and work, you haven't had a decent meal all week. So I thought maybe you'd like to go out and grab a bite. You name the place."

"Really?" It sounded too good to be true. There had to be a catch.

But there wasn't. He told me again to pick a place, any place. I knew exactly where I wanted to go — a place I'd eaten at for the first time with Riel. A little plain-looking restaurant down on Queen Street where they made ribs that reminded me of my mother's cooking. Riel smiled when I told him. It was his favourite place too.

"Come on," he said, turning, which is why he didn't see Mr. Henderson. He didn't, but I did. Mr. Henderson was standing on the landing halfway down the stairs from the second floor. He was looking at Riel. Looking at him the same way he had looked at Emily Corwin. What was *that* all about?

* * *

It wasn't until I was getting undressed later that I remembered the plastic bag from the drugstore. I pulled it out of my pocket. There was nothing inside except a sales slip. I started to crumple it up, then decided to look at it first. It was a sales slip from a drugstore for two items: contact lens solution and hair dye.

CHAPTER EIGHT

Emily wasn't going to be happy, but I had tried. I had done what she wanted me to do. The next day after school, I called her on the number she had given me and left a message. Then I did my homework and had supper with Riel. I was cleaning up when the doorbell rang.

A cop was standing on the front porch. A cop I knew, and not just because he was an old friend of Riel's. His name was Detective Jones and he grinned at me when I opened the door.

"Hey, Mike, relax," he said. "I'm here for John this time, not you. He here?"

"He went to the store," I said.

"You expect him back soon?"

"In a couple of minutes, I guess." Riel had this idea that a growing boy — me — needed plenty of milk. He poured me a big glass every morning, whether I wanted it or not, then made me drink it by telling me no way was he going to waste it by pouring it down the sink. We were out. He'd gone to get more.

"Mind if I come in and wait for him?" Detective Jones said. "It's cold out here."

I stepped aside to let him in.

"You better take your boots off," I said.

Detective Jones grinned again. "John," he said. "He's like Felix Unger. We used to tease him all the time that he probably had his sock drawer organized by colour." He thought that was pretty funny. I thought it was probably pretty accurate.

"I have to finish the dishes," I said.

Detective Jones pulled off his boots. He left them on the mat in the front hall, followed me through the living room and dining room, pausing to look around.

"Nice," he said, nodding at the dining room table. "New?"

"A couple of weeks," I said. Susan had helped Riel pick it out. He didn't have much furniture, considering how long he had been living in the house, but what he had was good stuff. You pick it right, he said, it'll last a lifetime.

When he got to the kitchen, Detective Jones looked at the pile of dishes soaking in the sink.

"You guys need a dishwasher," he said.

I agreed. But Riel didn't trust dishwashers. He didn't think they cleaned things well enough. But I didn't say that. I just shrugged and plunged my hands into the hot soapy water.

"Aw, what the heck," Detective Jones said. "I'll dry." He grabbed a towel from the rack at the end of the counter. "So, how's John treating you?"

"Okay, I guess," I said. "Glasses go in that cupboard."

He found the cupboard okay, but put the glass he'd just dried on the wrong side of the shelf. Geeze, the guy was a detective. Didn't he notice that the tall glasses, what Riel called the water glasses, were all on the right, and the small glasses, the juice glasses, were on the left? I was going to have to redo everything he was doing. Either that or I'd have to watch Riel do it the next time he opened the cupboard. And he'd be grousing at me the whole time.

Detective Jones had put a couple more glasses into the cupboard more or less at random and had moved over to messing up the side plates and the saucers when I heard the front door open.

"Mike?" Riel's voice. "Is someone here?"

Detective Jones threw the dishtowel onto the counter. Riel appeared in the doorway, his parka still on, a jug of milk — organic — in one hand.

"Hey, Jonesy," he said, surprised. He glanced at me, like maybe I was the reason his friend had showed up unexpectedly.

"I need to talk to you, John," Detective Jones said. "You got a minute?"

"Sure," Riel said. He put the milk into the fridge and then frowned when he spotted the dishtowel Detective Jones had dropped onto the counter. He picked it up, folded it and hung it on the towel rack. "What's up?"

"You heard about that body they found up in Caledon?" Detective Jones said.

"In the woods? Yeah, I saw it in the paper. They get an ID on it yet?"

Detective Jones shook his head. "We're still working on it."

"*We?*" Riel said. "Doesn't Peel have it?" He meant the Peel Regional Police. Detective Jones was with the Toronto Police Service. "Or is it OPP?"

"Technically, the body was in the village of Snel-grove, so, technically, it's Peel," Detective Jones said. "So we're *cooperating*."

"You mean, you want in and they're trying to decide whether they'll let you," Riel said. Detective Jones shrugged. "How come? What's it to you?"

"The guy was shot," Detective Jones said.

"I heard."

"We don't know who he is yet, but one thing we do know. The bullet that killed him? It came out of the same gun that killed Tracie Howard."

The colour drained from Riel's face, boom, like his head was a paint can and someone had just shot a hole in the bottom of it. Detective Jones reached for him.

"You okay, John?"

Riel didn't say anything.

Detective Jones grabbed a chair from the kitchen table and swung it over so that it was right behind Riel.

"You better sit down," he said. He looked at me. "You got homework, Mike?"

"I haven't finished the dishes yet," I said.

"They can wait," Detective Jones said. "Maybe you can find something else to do right now."

I hesitated. I wanted to know what was going on. Then Riel found his voice.

"*Now*, Mike," he said.

I left the rest of the dishes in the sink and cleared out of the kitchen. Detective Jones closed the door behind me. I knew he would be listening for me to go upstairs. They both would. I had no choice. I climbed the stairs to wait until Detective Jones left or it was time to go to the community centre — whichever came first.

Detective Jones didn't stay long — maybe ten minutes more. When I heard the kitchen door open again, I crept away from the top of the stairs into the darkness of the upstairs hall.

"I just thought you'd want to know," Detective Jones said. "We're going to try to keep it under wraps for a few days at least, see if we can find Howard before the media gets hold of it. But they *are* going to get hold if it, John, probably sooner rather than later. You know how they are. I wanted you to hear about it before you see it on the eleven o'clock news."

"I appreciate that," Riel said. There was a long pause before he said, "You have any idea where Howard is?"

"I heard he went out west after he was acquitted. We're in touch with police services out there. We're looking for him."

I waited a few more minutes after Detective Jones left. Then I went downstairs. Riel was in the kitchen. He'd finished the dishes and was straightening out the cupboards that Detective Jones had messed up. I got the milk out of the fridge, an excuse to ask him to please pass me a glass, which he did silently. Then I asked, "Who's Tracie Howard?"

Riel folded the dishtowel that he had slung over his shoulder while he straightened the cupboard. He hung it on the towel rack. "She's a woman who was murdered," he said.

I waited, but he didn't tell me anything else. "Did you know her?" I said.

"I worked on the case."

"When you were in homicide."

"Yeah," he said. "When I was in homicide."

"Did you get whoever did it?"

Riel isn't exactly a laugh-a-minute guy at the best of times. He's the serious type. He's also the type of guy who doesn't waste words. But he was more serious than usual tonight and he was paying out his words the way a miser pays out pennies, one at a time, letting each one go reluctantly.

"They eventually arrested a guy," he said.

They? "I thought you said you worked on the case."

He looked over at the window for a moment. Then he said, "It's a long story, Mike. The short version is, a guy was eventually arrested. Something like eighteen months after that, he went to trial. By the time it was over, he'd been acquitted." He glanced up at the clock above the kitchen table. "I have essays to mark," he said. "Don't you have to get to work?"

* * *

Riel was sitting at the dining room table when I got home, but he wasn't marking essays. From the number of empty beer bottles sitting on the table

— five empties in front of a guy who normally drank only one beer — I'd have bet he hadn't read even a single essay.

"Everything okay?" I said.

"Go to bed, Mike."

His face looked strained. His eyes were watery. He reminded me of Billy when he'd had too much to drink.

"You know, because if there's anything — "

Anger flashed in his eyes. It scared me. I'd seen him annoyed before. Disappointed. Frustrated. Even impatient, although that was rare. But angry? Never.

"I mean it, Mike. Go to bed."

I backed off and went up to my room. I sat down on my bed and wondered if I should call Susan. Something was definitely wrong. If Riel didn't want to talk to me, fine. He didn't know me all that well. Besides, I was just a kid — at least, that's probably how he looked at it. But Susan was his friend. Maybe more than that. Maybe she could help talk to him about whatever was bothering him.

I didn't call her, though. Instead, I got changed, climbed into bed and sat there for a while, reading — well, trying to concentrate on reading, but really I was listening for Riel to come upstairs. I guess I fell asleep because the next thing I knew it was two in the morning and I could see from under my door that the lights were still on downstairs.

I got up and tiptoed out into the hall. The door to Riel's bedroom was still open, which told me that he hadn't gone to bed yet. I went downstairs.

He was sitting exactly where I'd left him a few hours before. The only difference was that there were seven empty beer bottles in front of him now instead of five and he had an eighth in his hand that he was working on. His eyes were even glassier now.

"Go back to bed, Mike," he said, without even looking at me. He sounded like he meant business too, using that tone that was half-cop, half-teacher, half-guardian, half-drill-sergeant.

"It's two o'clock," I said.

He lifted the beer bottle he was holding and drank from it.

"You have school tomorrow," I said.

He put the bottle down again, but otherwise didn't move.

I sat down at the end of the table, opposite him. That got a reaction. He stood up. I noticed that he was a little unsteady on his feet.

"Go back to bed," he said. This time he shouted the words at me, really angry now, or trying to scare me, or both.

I stayed put. He thought because he was a teacher who bossed kids around all day and because he used to be a cop and used to wear a gun and could arrest people if they didn't do what they were told, that he could bully me. He forgot that I used to live with Billy. He forgot that I had a pretty good idea what drinkers were like and that I wasn't afraid of them.

"The reason you quit being a cop, does it have something to do with this woman who was murdered, Tracie Howard?" I said. "Billy said it was because you got shot and your partner got killed, but that isn't the whole reason, is it?"

He stood at the other end of the table, swaying a little and holding onto the back of a chair to keep himself steady.

"You don't want to tell me, fine," I said. "Maybe I'll call Susan and ask her. Or maybe your friend Detective Jones would fill me in if I asked him. Or maybe there was something about it in the papers. I'm not stupid, you know. I know how to use a library." Well, I knew how to ask a reference librarian for help — I'd seen Rebecca do it a few times.

He held tight to the chair and looked down at the table. He didn't say anything. I started to get a bad feeling. I had lived with Riel for a couple of months now. I thought I had a fix on him. He didn't talk about himself all that much, but he was good at school, up at the front of the classroom. And he always insisted we sit down to supper together and he'd ask me about what I had learned or how things were going with my job or with Sal or Rebecca, if I had heard from Vin and how he was doing, that kind of stuff. He gave me the impression that he really was interested, he wasn't just going through the motions. Sure, he was strict. If I didn't do what I was supposed to, I'd get a lecture. But he lightened up whenever Susan was around. He took her out at least once a week and at least once a week she'd come over or he'd go over to her place. When he did, he always came back late. If I was up when he got back, I'd see a smile on his face. But I had never seen him like he was now. Now he was like a whole different person. A stranger.

"Fine," I said. I stood up. "But I gotta tell you, you're a real hypocrite. You're always telling me, you got a problem, talk it out. Trust someone. Guess that only applies to other people, huh? Guess it doesn't apply to you."

I got nothing. No reaction. Fine. I shoved the chair back into the table and went upstairs again.

I lay in bed wondering if he was going to sit down there drinking all night. I wondered if he was the kind of guy who, once he got good and started, just kept on drinking. That was something else I didn't know about him. And that scared me too. Up until now I'd figured, sure, he could be a real pain with all his rules and clean this and clean that. But I always had the feeling I could count on him. Now I wasn't so sure.

I don't know how long it was before the light went on in the hall and I heard him come up the stairs. It seemed like forever. Then I heard it — a knock on my door and his voice, quiet.

"Mike, you still awake?"

I thought about not answering. But then I said, "Yeah, I'm awake."

The door stayed closed and he stayed on the other side of it.

"Can I talk to you for a minute?" he said.

I said, sure. I told him, come in.

He pushed open the door, but didn't switch on the overhead light. When I sat up and reached for the lamp next to my bed, he said, "Leave it off, okay?" He pulled out the chair from my desk and sat down.

"I want to apologize for how I behaved," he said. "I should know better."

I didn't say anything. I knew there was more coming. If all he'd wanted to do was apologize, he would have stayed at the door. Instead he had come in and sat down.

"Tracie Howard left two children when she was murdered," he said. "One was twelve, the other was eight. They were from Tracie's first marriage. When Tracie was murdered, she and the kids were living with Tracie's second husband, a guy named Tom Howard. Tom Howard was the main suspect in her murder. He and Tracie had been arguing a lot — the neighbours said they heard them. They also said Tom had a real temper. He had no alibi for when it happened. He was having money problems and Tracie had a nice insurance policy. When she died, Tom collected a lot of money — well, for a guy with his earning potential."

I could see his eyes looking at me from the shadows.

"Tom said Tracie had been getting phone calls. Threatening phone calls. He said she called him at work one time, hysterical because someone had tried to break into the house. He said she didn't know who the guy was, he was a stranger. He said after the guy was at the house, Tracie found her cat dead in the backyard. Eviscerated. You know what that is?"

I nodded.

"Funny thing, though. Tom was never home when Tracie got the calls. And from what we were able to find out, all the calls came from a couple of pay phones near where Tom worked. And the cat? Tom said Tracie buried it in the backyard. If she did, we never found it. She didn't tell her kids about any of this either. They said their mom told them Ginger — that was the cat's name — Ginger ran away. You can see how none of this made Tom Howard look too good. You can see it, right?"

I said I could.

"One time when we talked to him, he said the kids were scared. He said every time they heard a car come by the house, they got scared someone was going to come and shoot them the way their mother was shot. The older one in particular. She was the one who came though the door first that night — she and her sister had gone to a friend's house after school and the friend's mother dropped them off. The older one was first through the door. She was the one who found her mother." He paused a moment, squeezed his eyes shut and then opened them again. "Tracie Howard was shot four times. Twice in the head, twice in the chest. There was an awful lot of blood and not a whole lot of face left. You understand what I'm saying?"

I said I did.

"So the older kid, the one who found her, was pretty traumatized. And what she heard from Tom and from the neighbours, probably from the TV at first too, was that a stranger had killed her mother. Tom kept telling us how scared she was. Said she woke up every night with nightmares. Said she even wet her bed one time. Couldn't stand to be alone anywhere, especially in the house. That kind of thing."

I had a pretty good idea how she felt.

"Tom Howard was pretty high-strung himself," Riel said. He was talking slowly, carefully. It reminded me of the way Billy used to talk when he'd had too much to drink but was trying to make you think that he hadn't, that he had it all under control. "He was mad at the police because we were investigating him. He showed up at the police station and caused a real disturbance. He was lucky he wasn't arrested for that. Another time we went out to the house to talk to him and he blew up at us. Told us that unless we had a warrant, we could get off his property and stop scaring his kids. It took a lot of talking to get him calmed down, to make him see how he wasn't helping himself any."

He stopped for a moment and looked down at the floor. He shook his head slowly. Then he said, "One day we had to go out to the house again, ask him one more thing, you know, like detectives are always doing on TV. Marty — that was my partner at the time, Marty Tennant. A good cop. Seven years on the job, new to homicide. Marty knocked on the door. We were doing it by the book, being cautious, you know. Marty was on one side of the door, I was on the other, you know, because Tom could get pretty excited when cops were around. Marty knocked on the door and the next thing you know, we heard a scream. It sounded like one of the kids, so Marty goes for the door." Riel shook his head slowly. "The way they make it seem later, when they're asking all those questions — did you do this, did you do that — they make it seem like you've got all the time in the world to think. But you don't. The whole thing took, I don't know, five, maybe ten seconds. I see Marty move in front of the door, like he's going to open it. I open my mouth to say who we are. I remember that because I remember thinking that's what Marty should have done, he should have identified us. But before I could say anything, *BLAM!* Right through the door — a shotgun blast and Marty goes flying backward. He's down, you understand? Caught it right in the chest. We just wanted to talk to the guy and he's shooting at us." Riel's voice faded for a moment. He looked down at the floor again when he continued. "I think about it now and it's like one of those kids' toys. A kaleidoscope. You know, all those pieces, all shifting around. Marty's on the ground and there's blood everywhere. Someone inside opens the door and I see the barrel of a shotgun. That's it, just the barrel, pointing at me and I yell, Drop it. But I still see it pointing at me so I shoot. Then someone screams. Then there's another shot and I'm down."

He looked up at me.

"I didn't even know what happened until a couple of days later. I woke up in the hospital and before too long my boss is standing there. He tells me that Marty's dead. He tells me that Tom Howard shot me. Then he tells me that Tom Howard didn't shoot Marty. It was his step-daughter who did it — Tracie's older kid, the twelve-year-old. She heard our car pull up, but she didn't recognize who we were and we never identified ourselves. She panicked. She thought we were going to kill her. So she grabbed the shotgun. She's twelve years old, you understand? I didn't even know she could lift the thing, let alone shoot it. And the reason Tom shot me is . . . is that the girl was still holding the shotgun when I saw it. I shot her. Tom says after I shot her, he believed I was going to shoot him too. He said he was defending himself, his home and his family."

Geeze.

"Not that it matters what was going through his head," Riel said. "It all comes down to the same thing. Marty was dead and I shot the little girl. Left her a quadriplegic — paralysed from the neck down. That was it for me. I never went back to homicide. When I got back on my feet, I transferred to traffic services, the detective office there. I heard the girl died last year. Tom Howard was eventually tried for Tracie's murder. When he was acquitted . . . " Riel's voice trailed off. He shrugged. "I wasn't very effective after that. I decided, maybe I should do something else with my life."

Something like become a teacher.

"They never made another arrest in the Tracie Howard murder. Except now they have another guy killed with the same gun that killed Tracie. Okay?"

Okay? What did that mean?

He stood up, crossed to the door and hung there for a moment, looking at me.

"I'm sorry," he said. "I should be acting more responsibly."

"You're doing okay," I said. "Considering."

He leaned forward, out of the shadows and into the light from the hall. I saw him smile just a little. "The press will eventually get hold of this," he said. "They'll dredge it all up. You understand that, right?"

I said I did. I didn't know what else to say.

After he left my room, I lay there thinking about how I had seen the scar on his chest one time and, before that, what Billy had told me. Billy had said Riel quit being a cop after his partner was killed. That part was more or less right, even though it didn't happen as fast as Billy had made it sound, but it wasn't close to being the whole story. Billy had said that Riel's partner had busted down an apartment door, that Riel was supposed to be backing him up, that Riel had frozen, that he hadn't fired a single shot. That was all wrong. All of it. I should have known. Billy always got things wrong.

He probably had it all confused with about a million cop shows and cop movies he'd watched. The way Billy had told it, Riel had come off looking like a coward. That wasn't right either. One thing about Billy's version, though — thinking about it now, it seemed to me like it would be easier for Riel if what Billy had said were true. It'd be easier for him to blame himself for being a coward than to live with the fact he had shot a twelve-year-old girl and left her paralysed.

CHAPTER NINE

If it were TV instead of real life, the whole story would have been splashed across the front page of the newspaper the next day. But I scanned every headline on every page — even the little headlines in the "In brief" columns, and found no mention of the body they had found in the woods, no mention of Tracie Howard, no mention of John Riel.

Riel woke me up at the same time he usually did. His face was pale and his eyes were puffy, and he drank two cups of coffee instead of his usual one while I ate my granola, but other than that he seemed okay.

I didn't say anything to Sal or Rebecca about what had happened. It didn't seem right to tell them something that had been so hard for Riel to tell me. At lunchtime I headed for the pay phone in the cafeteria and dialled the number for Emily's cell phone. She picked up on the second ring.

"How come you didn't call me back sooner?" she said, sounding mad.

"Something came up."

"Well?" she said. "Did you get anything?"

"Not much," I said.

She wanted to know what I *had* got, exactly, so I told her about the coloured contact lenses and the hair dye. She liked that.

"So the guy has changed the colour of his eyes and the colour of his hair," she said. "What do you think, he's a fugitive from justice?"

Yeah, right. I was getting the idea that Emily liked to make things exciting, liked to pretend she was living in a TV show.

"What else?" Emily said. "Where does he live? Is he married?"

"I don't know."

"Find out," she said. It came out like an order. "Find out and I'll give my wallet to you instead of taking it to the police. Come over to my house tomorrow, one o'clock."

"I work until one."

"So come at two. You can do that, right, McGill?" Pushing me now with that rich-girl way of talking she had.

"Yeah," I said. "I'll be there."

"Be where?" said a voice behind me. I almost dropped the phone and, of course, Rebecca noticed that. She also noticed the nervous, guilty look on my face that I was working hard to hide. I dropped the receiver back onto its cradle. "Who were you talking to?" she said. Only instead of sounding casual about it, like she was interested but not dying of curiosity, she sounded the way my mom would have if she'd caught me doing something I shouldn't have been doing. And stupid me, all of a sudden I acted like I was five instead of fifteen.

I said, "No one. It's nothing."

Rebecca did the same thing my mother would have done in the same situation. She crossed her arms over her chest, tilted her head to one side, looked hard at me, and said, "You were talking to *no one*?"

"No one important," I said. Then I smiled at her and said, "You look great." I reached for her hand. She snapped it away from me.

"You were talking to no one important who, I suppose, you're planning to meet nowhere," she said. "Or should that be nowhere *important*?"

Okay, now I had to decide whether the best way out of this was to get angry — hey, it's *my* life, *my* business, geeze, *my* personal, private phone call — or to apologize and, what the heck, tell her the truth. Except I had this picture in my mind of what would happen if I told her that I'd been talking to Emily Corwin, who, let's face it, Rebecca hated. I'd say, I'm going over to Emily's place tomorrow, no big deal. And, of course, Rebecca wouldn't let me leave it at that. She would want the whole truth. She'd want to know why I was going there. Then I'd have to tell her what had happened the last time I was there — and she would want to grill me on that, exactly why I'd gone there, exactly what I'd done there and, most importantly, why I hadn't told her about it. I'd try to keep her focused on what had happened with the wallet, that Emily had taken me up to her room — how she'd made sure the housekeeper knew I had gone up there — and had shown me those earrings, how she threatened to say I had stolen them too, how she was having a whole lot of fun getting me to do whatever she wanted. But I knew what Rebecca would fix on: You were in her *room*? You were in Emily Corwin's *bedroom*? And, boy, would she be mad about that. And, let's face it, I couldn't really blame her. I'd react the same way if I found out she'd been in some guy's bedroom. It doesn't matter how innocent it is, it never sounds that way to someone who wasn't there, especially when that someone already hates the person whose bedroom it is.

"Really, it's nothing," I said. "It's just a thing I have to do. For Riel."

"Oh," she said, her voice as tight as the arms she had crossed in front of her chest. "You were talking to Mr. Riel on the phone?" She turned her head a little and nodded toward the door to the cafeteria where Riel was standing, talking to another teacher or being talked at by another teacher.

"No," I said. "Of course not. I just — "

"You just don't feel like being honest with me," she said. "Okay." Meaning that it was *not* okay. "Fine." Meaning that it was *not* fine. "If that's the way you want it." Meaning it sure wasn't the way *she* wanted it. "I have to go."

"Hey, Rebecca." I made a grab for her and caught her arm. She gave me a sharp look and jerked free of me.

"I have to go," she said again, and then she was off across the cafeteria, elbowing her way out the door, not caring who she shoved, not even seeming to hear when some kid said, "Hey, watch it!" and Riel looked to see what was going on and saw it was Rebecca. He frowned. He kept on frowning while he swept the cafeteria to see what had provoked her and found me, still standing beside the pay phone. Probably still looking guilty.

* * *

Susan came over just before I left to go to the community centre. She had a bag of groceries in one hand and a bottle of wine in the other when I opened the door for her.

"I'm making chicken tikka," she said. Susan was a good cook, always putting together something interesting and never making a big deal about whether or not it was organic. "I'll save you some."

"He isn't home yet," I said.

She looked — what? — disappointed? No, that wasn't it. They'd been spending time together since before I knew Riel. So she didn't act like she thought he was standing her up. No, it was more that she looked worried.

"He's running late, I guess," she said. "I'm going to get things started. Okay?" Like I had any say in the matter. It wasn't my house. Still, I followed her into the kitchen and watched her put the bottle of wine into the fridge to chill. I thought about talking to her about what had happened last night. She was smiling when she closed the fridge and turned to unpack the groceries she had brought. When she looked at me, her smile faded. "Is everything okay, Mike?" I wasn't sure why she had turned so serious all of a sudden.

"Yeah," I said. I decided right then not to say anything. It was none of my business. If Riel wanted to talk to Susan about it, he would. Maybe she already knew, maybe that's why she was here and why she had that look on her face. Maybe she'd known the whole story all along. "I better get to work," I said.

While I was walking to the community centre, I didn't think about Riel. Instead I thought about how I was going to find out where Mr. Henderson lived and what Emily was going to do with that information. She was a weird girl. She looked nice and sweet and normal, but she wasn't. She was bossy and edgy and a little bit scary. Mr. Henderson had been staring at her. He had gone into her wallet. But instead of doing what any normal person would have done, instead of telling her dad or telling the cops, Emily wanted to get back at him herself. She wanted to teach him a lesson. What was that all about?

Mr. Henderson was standing in the main floor hall when I got to the community centre. I tried the direct approach first — well, as direct as a person can get with someone like him. He looked at me, not smiling — I don't think he ever smiled — when I came through the door. I asked him if he had anything special he needed me to do, any rooms to set up for events the next day, any special cleaning assignments.

"Mop the third floor," he said. "Then the second floor — "

"Then the ground floor," I said. "Got it." Same old same old. I followed him upstairs.

"You know," I said as I climbed the stairs with him, "I think I've spent more time here because I had to than I ever did because I wanted to. This place is all right. There's always something going on. You live around here, Mr. Henderson?"

He turned to look at me. "What does that have to do with anything?"

"Just wondering," I said. Geeze, he was prickly. "You know, because I live pretty close and I never realized this place was so — " So what? "So busy."

He gave me another look, like maybe I wasn't too bright. "I work here. I can see how busy it is by how busy it keeps me."

Okay, so he wasn't going to tell me where he lived. "You married, Mr. Henderson?" I said. "You have kids?"

He didn't answer. He reached the top of the stairs and limped down the hall to the utility closet. He unlocked it and then paused to glance at me before he turned the knob.

"That guy I saw you with the other night," he said.

What guy? Had he seen me with Sal? Or — wait a minute — did he mean Riel?

"What guy?" I said.

"Tall guy. Dark hair. He's not your father, is he?" He asked the question like he was pretty sure of the answer already.

"No."

"But you live with him, right?"

He must have asked about Riel. Maybe he had

talked to Teresa Rego. She knew that Riel was responsible for me. It was the only way I could think of that Mr. Henderson already knew about Riel and me.

"Yeah," I said. "He's my foster parent."

"Where are your own parents?"

"Dead."

He looked at me, but didn't say anything. He opened the closet and stepped aside to let me go in. I felt him watching me as I lifted the bucket from its frame, set it into the sink, measured out some soap and turned on the hot water tap.

"Dead how?" he said after a while.

"My father in a car accident," I said. Then, because I didn't want to talk about it, I said, "My mother too."

I guess nobody had told him that. Surprise registered in his eyes. He looked at me a little longer and I looked right back at him. Then he said, "I'm not married. No kids. No family at all." I had the feeling that he was thinking: just like you.

* * *

I mopped the third floor — again. The old part, where the fire had been, was boarded off. They were still cleaning it up. It had got to the point that I knew the halls of the community centre better than I knew my own room. I emptied the bucket, rinsed the mop and closed the third-floor utility closet. Then I went down to the second floor. Mr. Henderson was already at the door, unlocking it. He limped away without saying a word. The same thing happened when I finally reached the first floor. I mopped down one corridor and then started on another. I was coming around a third side of the big square when I saw Teresa Rego standing in front of a bulletin board. She smiled when she saw me and asked me how things were going.

"Okay, I guess," I said.

"Mr. Henderson isn't giving you a hard time, I hope," she said.

I shrugged. "He's okay," I said. "He sure has his own way of doing things, though."

She laughed and said, "I'll say. But the place has never been cleaner than it has been in the past . . . let me see . . . I guess it's almost six months now."

"Mr. Henderson has only worked here for six months?" I don't know why, but he seemed like a lifer to me.

"He started coming here as a volunteer," she said, "working with the aqua-therapy group." The Wednesday evening group. "He'd just arrived in town and was looking for work, and when our old janitor quit, well, I hired him on the spot. He's gruff, but he's thorough. And he's great with the kids in aqua-therapy."

"Does he live around here?"

She gave me a funny look. "That I don't know," she said. "He never said and, to be honest, I never asked. Mr. Henderson likes to keep to himself." Now she gave me a teacher look, trying to see if I understood what she was saying. I went back to my mopping. I wondered if Emily would trade the wallet for the piece of information Teresa had just given me and the few tidbits Mr. Henderson had revealed. Somehow I doubted it.

CHAPTER TEN

After work the next day I took the subway uptown, transferred to a bus and then walked from the bus stop to Emily's house. This time after Estelle the housekeeper buzzed me through the front gate and I rang the doorbell, it wasn't Emily who answered. It was her dad. Even if I hadn't run into him before, I would have guessed who he was from the way he looked — tanned, perfect teeth perfectly white, a not-a-single-hair-out-of-place-blow-dried haircut, chinos with a crease in them you could cut yourself on, a sweater that looked baby soft (my guess: cashmere), a wafer-thin watch that probably cost a couple of grand, a thick gold ring with a great big sparkly diamond on the third finger of his right hand. Oh yeah, and in his right earlobe, a diamond stud. Emily had said that on a guy his age, it didn't look cool, it looked stupid. Personally, I liked it. He had style.

He looked me over pretty good too. Looked at my navy blue parka that was hanging open, my Boca sweatshirt underneath, my faded jeans, my twenty-dollar watch, my scuffed sneakers instead of boots (I had boots, I just didn't like to wear them unless there was actually snow on the ground). He reminded me of Jen's dad. He used to look at me the same way, like he was adding up how little I was worth compared to him — and Jen's dad wasn't nearly as loaded as Emily's dad.

"May I help you?" he said.

May. He didn't sound stuffy, though. Instead he sounded, well, correct. Like he was trying to be polite, even though he didn't look remotely like a guy who would ever dirty his hands helping someone like me.

"I'm here to see Emily," I said.

He didn't smile. He didn't stand aside to let me in. He didn't call Emily. He just stared at me. Yup, he was Jen's dad all over again.

"And you are . . . ?" He acted like he didn't recognize me.

I told him my name.

He peered at me again. I felt like something he had plopped onto a slide and slid under a microscope, the way we had to do in biology class. Something from a swamp, maybe, or a sewer. Some slimy little life form.

"Do I know you?" he said.

The question kind of threw me. Did he know me? I'd pulled him off a guy in the street. I'd told him someone had called the cops on him. But maybe he hadn't paid any attention to me. He'd been pretty focused on Neil, and had hardly even looked my way when I'd tried to grab his arm.

"I'm a friend of Emily's," I said.

"And may I ask how you know her?"

"From swimming," I said, which was true. "She invited me — "

And then there was Emily saying, "Dad, you promised — no more third degree." She reached

116

around her father, grabbed my hand and pulled me inside. "Mike and I will be out on the deck," she said. She pulled me inside and away from her father.

The deck turned out to be the deck of a swimming pool that was completely glassed-in.

"Wow, you can swim here in the winter," I said. If Rebecca had been there, she would have kicked me. I sounded totally in awe.

"The roof retracts," Emily said, "for when you want to swim outside."

"In summer, you mean?" I said.

"In winter, too. The pool's heated. You ever been swimming outside in a heated pool in February, McGill? It's nice."

I bet it was.

She sat down at a round table on the deck. Her wallet was sitting on it, still inside the plastic bag. "So," she said, "what did you find out?"

"Not much." I told her the scraps of information I had gathered — that Mr. Henderson was relatively new in town, that he volunteered to help disabled kids, that he kept pretty much to himself, that he had no family.

Emily listened. She seemed irritated by how little I was able to tell her. She looked at the wallet. "You really knocked yourself out, huh?" she said.

She sounded exactly like half the teachers I'd ever had, teachers who think that if you don't get an A-plus on a test or an assignment or an essay, it's because you didn't try. She made a pouty face and looked over at the pool.

"Hey, Emily?" I said. She turned her dark brown eyes on me. "You want someone to do errands for you, why don't you ask Neil?"

"Neil?" She sounded surprised. "Neil has nothing to do with me. Neil's from before."

Before? "Before what?"

"Before I came back here," she said, "where I belong. I asked you to do something, McGill, for your own good."

"Do I look like a detective to you?" I said. And then, I don't even know why, I glanced at the wall of glass that separated the pool from the house and I thought maybe I was seeing things, because there, on the other side of the glass, talking to Emily's father, were two detectives. Police detectives. Detective Jones, who had been at Riel's house a couple of days ago, and his partner, Detective London. What was going on? What were they doing in Emily's house, talking to Emily's father?

Emily must have caught the look on my face, because she turned and looked through the glass and then turned back and looked at me.

"What?" she said.

"Nothing," I said, which I now know is the exact wrong word to say to a girl, unless, of course, you want to convince her that you're hiding something from her.

She looked at the two strangers talking to her father — strangers to her, that is. "You know those guys," she said. She was telling me, not asking me.

I'd been around Rebecca enough to know there was no point in lying.

When I told her they were cops, she took another look at them, really interested now.

"What kind of cops?" she said.

"Homicide."

Then, *boom*, just like that, her face changed. She didn't look so tough anymore. She didn't look so superior either. Instead she looked like a scared little kid. Who wouldn't, with homicide cops in her house, talking to her father?

"Homicide?" She didn't sound snotty or even cool anymore either. Her voice was small and full of surprise. "You sure?"

I nodded. Emily got up from the table. She didn't say anything, she didn't excuse herself, she just walked inside where her father was and then she stood there until the two detectives introduced themselves. For a moment, it looked like her father was trying to get her to leave, but she wouldn't. She said something to the detectives. It was Detective Jones who answered her, which didn't surprise me. In my experience, he was the nice one. The one who played good cop. Detective London liked to lean on people. He liked to make people sweat, liked to scare them even more. Riel said it was just an act. I wasn't so sure.

Emily started to shake her head, slowly at first and then faster. I saw her father reach out for her and try to pull her to him, but she shook her head even harder and wriggled free. Then she ran away.

I didn't see where she went. She didn't come outside again, so she must have gone somewhere in the house. Maybe upstairs to her room. Detective London turned in the direction she had gone. Detective Jones looked out through the glass and saw me. I know he did. He looked right at me, but there was no expression on his face. Then he shifted his attention back to Emily's father and said something to him.

I turned my head away from the glass and sat alone out beside the pool, wondering what I should do. There was a door that led out into the yard, but I didn't know if there was some way to get around the house and back out to the street without passing through some impossible-to-penetrate high-security gate. I waited, wondering if the cops were still there and if Emily was coming back and, if she wasn't, how I was going to get out of here. The wallet was still sitting in the middle of the table, still in its baggie. I looked at it. Then I picked it up and slipped it into the pocket of my parka.

After a moment I heard a door open behind me. I turned and saw Emily's father standing on the deck.

"I think you'd better go," he said, but not in a mean way. His face seemed pale, even with the tan. He looked a little stunned. "Emily's had — *we've* had — some bad news. She can't see anyone right now."

I wondered what was going on. It had to be something bad — no, the *worst* — if homicide cops were there. But I didn't get it. What had happened?

When I followed Mr. Corwin back into the house, I saw that the two detectives were gone. Mr. Corwin led me to the front door. He didn't say anything. He just opened the door and let me out.

I hadn't gone more than half a block when a car pulled up alongside me.

"Hey, Mike," Detective Jones said. "What a surprise running into you in this neighbourhood." In that house, he meant. In Emily's house. "Get in, why don't you? We'll give you a lift home."

I waited for him to unlock the door and then I climbed in. Detective London was driving. He glanced at me in the rearview mirror. He didn't speak to me, didn't smile at me the way Detective Jones sometimes did. I had the feeling he didn't like me. I said that to Riel once, but he said, "Nah, I don't think that's it. That's just the way Charlie is. Sees himself as one tough cop."

"Last I heard, Emily Corwin went to a private girls' school," Detective Jones said. "How come you know her, Mike?"

I got a cold-all-over feeling, like he knew something I wished he didn't. I wondered what Emily had said to him. Then I reminded myself that he was a homicide cop. Still, if Emily had told him that I'd stolen her wallet, he was guaranteed to be interested because he was a friend of Riel's.

"She's on a swim team," I said. "They have swim meets at the community centre where I work."

"Where you do community service, you mean,"

Detective London said. He glanced at me in the rearview mirror.

"It's still work," I said. "I just don't get paid for it."

"What were you doing at her house?" Detective Jones said.

"Nothing." Something I was making a career out of doing. "She asked me to come over."

Detective Jones turned in his seat to look at me. "I thought you were seeing that little redhead," he said. "What's her name?"

"Rebecca," I said. How did he know that? "I told you, I met Emily at the community centre. She asked me over. Why? What's the big deal?"

"Does John know you're acquainted with her?"

"With Emily, you mean? No." Did he think I told Riel every detail of my life?

"Emily ever talk to you about her mother?"

"No." Geeze, what was going on? Then I remembered what Rebecca had told me — that Emily's mother had died. And now here were two homicide cops showing up at her house. "What happened to her mother anyway?"

Detective Jones glanced at Detective London. Detective London looked at me in the rearview mirror again. Then Detective Jones turned in his seat again and said, "Her mother was Tracie Howard."

* * *

They drove me back to Riel's house. On the way Detective Jones asked me what I knew about Tracie Howard and about what had happened to Riel when he was on that case. I said that Riel had told me the whole story.

"Everything?" he said.

How was one person supposed to know if another person had told him everything?

"He told me about the girl he shot," I said. "He told me why he moved from homicide to traffic services and then why he quit."

Detective London stared straight ahead, like none of this had anything to do with him. I wondered what he thought of Riel — whether he liked him, the way his partner seemed to, or whether he thought Riel was a wuss, quitting the cops like he did.

Detective Jones shifted in his seat. "We went to see James Corwin to tell him about the connection between the body we found and his ex-wife. You know what that means, Mike?"

I wasn't sure what he was getting at.

"The media have it," he said. "It's going to be in the news." He peered hard at me. "John says you're doing okay. He says you had a hard time at first, but that you've settled in. In my opinion, he likes having you around."

Why was he telling me this?

"It's maybe going to be a little rough on John," he said. "You know how the media is. They get hold of something like this, *especially* something like this — unsolved murder, a kid shot, one cop dead, another one wounded. They're going to have a field day. You see what I'm saying, Mike?"

My stomach felt like it was tying itself into a great big knot. I saw exactly what he was saying. He was worried about Riel. And if he was worried . . .

He dug into his jacket pocket and handed me a business card. "I'm going to check in on John every now and again. But if anything happens you think I should know about, or if maybe you just want to talk to someone, give me a call, okay, Mike? Any time. I mean it."

I looked at him again. He was a couple of years older than Riel. A beefier guy with pale blue eyes and sandy brown hair that was starting to thin a little on top. I wondered if he'd ever been in a situation like Riel. I wondered if that's why he seemed to care so much. Or maybe he was the kind of guy who could imagine what it was like to be in a situation like that. Maybe he had more imagination than Detective London, who hadn't said a word about it, who hadn't looked at me the whole time Detective Jones was talking.

"Okay," I said. "Thanks."

* * *

Riel was down on his hands and knees in the kitchen, attacking the tile floor with a scrub brush.

"Gunk," he said, looking over his shoulder at me. "Gets in the cracks."

Right. I looked at the fridge, which was on the other side of a stretch of still-wet floor. It was nearly three in the afternoon. I hadn't eaten since morning.

"Where have you been?" Riel said, still scrubbing.

"Around," I said. I couldn't decide whether or not to tell him about Emily. "You okay?"

"Me?" He sounded surprised, like why would I even ask. "I'm fine. Rebecca called."

Oh. So maybe she wasn't still mad at me. I called her and she invited me over. When I hesitated, she said, "Unless you've got plans to do nothing."

I thought about what Detective Jones had said. I thought about Riel out in the kitchen, attacking the gunk. I thought about when the story would hit the media and how Riel would react and what, if anything — big *if* — I would be able to do about it.

"I'll be there," I said. And then I cleared it with Riel.

He nodded. He didn't quiz me. He kept right on scrubbing.

* * *

We were in Rebecca's family room. Rebecca was cuddled up on the couch next to me. She'd been nice to me ever since I got there. She hadn't actually apologized for walking out on me in the cafeteria, but she hadn't hinted around that I should apologize to her either, the way girls do when they're mad at you for something. She'd rented a couple of movies — an action movie and a kung-fu movie, the kind I liked and she didn't. She made sandwiches and milkshakes and later, when we were watching the movies, she made popcorn. So I guess that meant everything was okay.

At eleven o'clock I hit the pause button on the

VCR remote and flipped on the TV.

"What?" Rebecca said. "You don't like the movie?" We were watching the second video, the kung-fu one.

"I want to see the news," I said. "Okay?"

She nodded. If I'd wanted to watch the weather channel, I think she would have let me.

It was the second story. Rebecca stared at the TV. At first she didn't say anything. Then she said, "Did he say John Riel?" She came up off my shoulder and leaned closer to the TV screen. "Is that Mr. Riel?"

It was, just for a few seconds. A still shot of him up in the corner of the screen behind the announcer's head. Riel, with his hair a little shorter than it was now, and with a moustache, looking a little cockier than he did these days, looking almost like a know-it-all. And then there was Emily's father with his tan and his straight white teeth and his perfect hair, standing outside his house, talking into what looked like a couple of dozen microphones, saying what a scandal it was that his ex-wife's murderer was never brought to justice, what a crime it was that his older daughter was shot, how it was wrong, criminally wrong, that the police officer who shot her had never suffered any consequences. Boy, did he have that wrong.

Rebecca looked at me. "Mr. Riel shot a girl?" She sounded like she couldn't believe it.

"It was an accident," I said. Rebecca said something else to me, but I didn't hear it. I stood up.

"I have to go home," I said.

She didn't argue with me.

* * *

Riel was sitting in front of the TV in the living room. He looked at me when I came in, then turned his head back to the TV. I wanted to ask him if he was okay, but it seemed like such a dumb question. How okay would I be if I had done what he had done and now it was all over TV — for the second time? I thought maybe I should sit down with him. Maybe if I did, he would say something. But what could he possibly say? I stood there a moment, watching him as he listened to the sports news — or maybe he wasn't listening any more. Then I went upstairs to my room.

CHAPTER ELEVEN

I woke up early to the sound of the phone ringing. Three rings, but no voice, no one saying, hello. Then a minute or two of silence. Then three rings again. It was ringing through to voicemail, I realized.

A few minutes later the doorbell rang. Once. Twice. Three times. Four times. Geeze, and no one answered it.

I got out of bed and went downstairs. It was dark in the house. All of the blinds were still closed. Riel was standing in the dining room, holding his cell phone to his ear.

The doorbell rang again. I looked at him.

"You want me to get — "

He shook his head and held a finger to his lips. *Shh.*

The doorbell rang again.

Riel said something into the phone, and then he slipped the phone into his shirt pocket.

"It's the media," he said. "I don't want to talk to them, okay?"

"Okay."

"You go near the door or out the door and they'll be all over you," he said.

"So I'll stay inside. I've got homework. And my chores."

Riel looked at me for a moment. Then he said, "Thanks, Mike."

* * *

128

The doorbell rang and people hammered on the door for most of the morning. Then it got quiet. Riel peeked out one of the windows.

"They're still out there," he said. "A few of them anyway." He sounded discouraged. "I don't know. Maybe I should get it over with." But he didn't open the door and he didn't answer the phone, even though it kept ringing.

It was a long day.

Around six o'clock, Riel's cell phone rang. He answered it, but didn't say much. A few minutes later someone knocked on the door — it sounded like a code: two quick, two slow, two quick. Riel opened the door this time and let someone in. Detective Jones. I heard a voice behind him, asking a question. It was a reporter. Then someone else asked another question. Detective Jones thrust a paper bag at me, and then shut the door and locked it.

"How long have they been at it?" Detective Jones said to Riel.

"They started in first thing this morning."

"You talk to them?"

Riel shook his head.

"I brought dinner," Detective Jones said. He took the paper bag from me. "Chinese. You guys hungry?"

I sure was.

We went into the kitchen and Riel got out plates and cutlery and glasses while Detective Jones unpacked the food and set it out all over the table

— containers of beef and noodles, fried rice, egg rolls, cashew chicken, spareribs and vegetables, all steaming hot. He also had cans of pop for everyone — Coke for him and me, ginger ale for Riel. We sat down and ate.

"You saw Corwin on the news last night?" Detective Jones said after a bite of egg roll.

Riel nodded.

"Charlie and I went over to the house yesterday," he said. I tensed up. I wondered if he was going to mention that I'd been there. If he did, I wondered what Riel would say. But all he said was, "We were going back to the car after we talked to him and I told Charlie, I give him about two seconds to be on the phone to the papers. Remember what he was like when you were investigating the murder? Making statements every other day about how they must have scraped the bottom of the barrel when they assigned investigators to the case."

"Because we didn't arrest Tom Howard right away," Riel said. "Yeah, I remember. He kept saying it was obvious Howard had done it. What got to me — it wasn't like we weren't investigating Howard. My money's still on him."

"So how come he was acquitted?" I asked.

Detective Jones looked at Riel. Riel put down his fork.

"The whole case was circumstantial," he said. "Tom had a hot temper — he even admitted it. He and Tracie fought a lot, usually over money. He had no solid alibi. Said he was up at a cabin; but there was no evidence he'd been there, no one saw him. Said Tracie received threatening phone calls. But the times he gave us for when she got them, the only calls on record were from pay phones."

"In the neighbourhood where he worked," Detective Jones said.

"And he was the beneficiary of a sizeable amount of insurance money."

"When it finally paid out, it was quite a windfall," Detective Jones said. "Although I heard there was almost nothing left by the time he'd paid his legal bills."

"But if he had a motive and no alibi . . . " I said.

Riel shook his head. "We never found the weapon that was used. We never found any evidence of blood on any clothes Tom owned. We never found anything that tied him directly to the shooting."

Detective Jones took a swallow of Coke. "When John and Marty accused Tom Howard of making those calls himself, to set it up like Tracie was being threatened, Howard came up with another story. Right, John?"

Riel nodded. "He said maybe the phone calls — "

"And the cat," Detective Jones said. "Wasn't there supposed to have been a dead cat?"

"A dead cat we never found," Riel said. "So Howard changed his story. He said maybe the phone calls weren't related to the murder. He said some of her things were missing."

"What kind of things?" I said.

"Some jewellery," Detective Jones said.

"*All* of her jewellery," Riel said. "He said maybe someone broke into the house to rob it and was surprised to find Tracie there and killed her."

"Which the defence used," Detective Jones said. "Expensive jewellery was missing — "

"Which Tom probably took himself."

"And which we were never able to locate."

"The long and short of it, Mike, is that the Crown couldn't make its case beyond a reasonable doubt," Riel said. "So Howard was acquitted."

"Is that why James Corwin is so angry with the cops?" I said.

Detective Jones looked at Riel.

Riel said, "That and what happened to his daughter."

I was sorry I had asked.

"Now what happens?" I said.

Detective Jones looked across the table at me. "Now we concentrate on finding out who was buried out there in Caledon. Once we know that, we can maybe see how that links with Tracie Howard. In the meantime" — He dropped an egg roll onto his plate — "life goes on."

Riel looked down at his food for a moment. Then he said, "I need you to do me a favour, Dave."

Dave. Not Jonesy this time.

"Take Mike over to Susan's for me, would you?"

"*What?*" I said.

"I already talked to her," Riel said. He was looking at Detective Jones, not at me. "I should have done it as soon as you told me there was a link with

Tracie Howard's murder. I knew the press would be all over it. And I don't think that Mike should have to — "

"I don't want to go to Susan's," I said.

"Go pack a bag, Mike," Riel said.

"No."

Finally he turned to face me. "You have school tomorrow. I have school tomorrow. And they're going to be out there with their cameras and their microphones. I don't want you involved."

"I'm not going."

"Pack a bag or I'll pack it for you."

Like he was my father.

"Pack what you want, I'm not going," I said.

Riel looked at Detective Jones. Detective Jones shrugged. It looked like he didn't want to get involved. Riel turned back to me.

"They'll harass you, Mike. As soon as they find out who you are, they'll probably put that in the paper too, stuff about your mother and about Billy. You want that? You want your private life right there in the paper for everyone to read?"

"*Your* life's going to be in the paper."

"That's different. I was doing a job. You don't have to subject yourself to this."

"You're always telling me this is my home now. You're always saying I have responsibilities here, but I also have privileges, right? Isn't one of the privileges that I get to be here if I want to?"

"Come on, Mike."

"I want to stay."

Riel looked at Detective Jones again.

"He wants to stay," Detective Jones said. "But I have to go." He stood up and started putting the empty food containers into the paper bag he had brought the food in. "I'll stay in touch, John, let you know what's going on, okay?"

After he left, Riel said, "I better call Susan and tell her not to expect you."

That's all he said.

* * *

Riel had seemed pretty relaxed for a while when Detective Jones was at the house. He didn't seem nearly so relaxed the next morning. He was downstairs before me, as usual. As usual, he was packing his briefcase. What was different: he looked like he hadn't slept all night.

I peeked outside while I was drinking my milk. There was a TV van across the street and, a little ahead of it, a car with a man and a woman in it. The man was looking at the house. Other than that, it seemed quiet.

"Whatever they ask you, even if all they ask you is your name, you don't say anything, okay, Mike?" Riel said as he handed me my parka.

"Can I say, No comment?"

"It's better if you pretend you don't hear them and just say nothing at all."

He didn't say better for who, but if that's what he wanted me to do, that's what I was going to do.

I put on my backpack, he grabbed his briefcase and we went out the back door to the garage behind the house where his car was parked. By the time we got in it and Riel had turned the car around and was going down the laneway between his house and the one next door, two guys had got out of the TV van, one with a videocamera, the other with a microphone, and they were coming up the drive. The man and woman had got out of the other car too, and they were coming toward us, the woman holding out a small tape recorder. Then a few more people started up the driveway — I don't know where they came from — and they crowded around the car.

"Keep your head down, Mike," Riel said.

He kept inching the car forward, a little at a time so that the people in front of it had to keep moving back even though they didn't want to. Someone knocked on the driver's side window. Someone else rapped on my window. Riel didn't look to see who it was. He just kept edging the car forward. Then two police patrol cars pulled up across the street and four uniformed cops got out and came over and started moving the press away from Riel's car. One of them tapped on the window and this time Riel pressed the button to roll it down.

"You okay?" the cop asked.

Riel nodded.

"It's gonna be a long day," the cop said. He moved back and Riel cleared the driveway. As soon as he did, all the press ran for their cars and vans.

"They know where we're going," he said. "They'll probably be at school before we are."

They were.

There were cop cars down there too, keeping the media aside while Riel pulled into the underground parking and the door closed behind him. He pulled the key from the ignition and turned to me.

"You sure you don't want to stay with Susan for a couple of days, until things quiet down?"

I said I was sure.

"Or you could stay with Dave. You seem to get along okay with him. He lives alone."

"I want to stay at home with you," I said. Just like that, without even thinking about it. He caught the word at the same time I did — home — and nodded.

"Meet me here after school then," he said. "I think it would be better if we drove for the next little while."

I nodded, but didn't move.

"Go on in to school," Riel said.

"What about you?"

"They're not going to leave until they get what they want." He drew in a deep breath and then blew it out again. "I don't want them disrupting things here. I'm going to go out and talk to them."

"Yeah, but — "

"It's okay, Mike. It's not like I haven't done this before."

* * *

"Is it true?" Sal said. He came up and stood beside me at the windows along the catwalk that overlooked the school atrium inside and the street outside. Riel was out there, crushed in the middle of a bunch of reporters. There were uniformed cops on either side of him, looking out for him, I guess. I wondered if Detective Jones had anything to do with them being there.

I turned to look at Sal. His eyes shifted to the floor for a moment, then back up at me again. "I like him," he said. "He treats my father like he's normal. He one of the only people who does that."

"He likes your father," I said. Riel went to visit Sal's dad every couple of weeks. He always took along a book or a magazine in Spanish for Mr. San Miguel, and then he sat and talked to him, also in Spanish.

Sal said, "All I meant was, is he okay? Is anything bad going to happen?"

"Yeah, he's okay," I said, even though I wasn't entirely sure that was actually true. "I don't know what's going to happen. It was investigated after it happened." I meant the whole thing about the girl who was shot. Emily's sister — the one she hadn't wanted to talk about. No wonder. "It was ruled an accident. I don't think anything else is going to happen about that."

Sal gave me a look. He hadn't meant that at all. His dad had been in prison back in Guatemala where Sal's from. He was tortured while he was there and had never really recovered. So what Sal meant was, was Riel going to be okay with his past being made public, was he going to be okay coming into school and standing in front of four or five classes of kids every day, five days a week and then going into the staff lounge and being with all the teachers, and everyone knowing things about him that maybe they hadn't known before.

I wished I knew. But I didn't.

That day a lot of other people asked me the same thing that Sal had asked: *Is it true?* I just looked at them. I didn't answer.

I met Riel downstairs after school. I wanted to ask him if he was okay, but I could see that he wasn't. He looked tense and tired.

We got home okay — nobody bothered us — and I did my homework. Riel made supper, same as always, and then I headed to the community centre. I was almost at the main doors when a woman appeared out of nowhere and asked me if I was Michael McGill. I nodded. She asked me if I lived with John Riel. Who *was* she? How did she know my name? How did she know about Riel? Then she said, "The same John Riel who was a police detective with traffic services and who investigated your mother's death?" At the same time that she was asking me that, a guy appeared behind her and pointed a light and a camera at me, practically blinding me. I remembered what Riel had said — if they ask you any questions, don't say anything.

"Detective Riel botched that investigation too, didn't he?" the woman said.

I tried to back away from her, but she kept shoving her microphone in my face and the guy with the camera kept his light steady on me. Then someone grabbed my arm. I started to jerk free, but saw that it was Teresa Rego.

"Come on, Mike," she said. She pulled me toward the door. The woman with the camera was still moving forward, still trying to get me to say something. "Aren't you ashamed of yourself?" Teresa asked her. "He's just a kid." She got me inside the community centre and then into her office. She locked the door. "Well," she said, sinking down on the chair behind her desk, "now I've got to figure out how to get you out of here again."

"Maybe they'll just go away," I said.

"Those people never go away." She sounded like maybe she had some experience with the press. Bad experience. She looked at me. "Is John at home?"

"I think so."

She called Riel and told him what was going on. She listened for a minute and then she passed the phone to me.

"Sit tight," Riel said. "I'll get someone to pick you up."

I thought maybe it would be Detective Jones but, no, it was Susan. First I saw her car slide up the driveway that ran alongside the community centre and led to the parking lot in the back. Then the phone rang in Teresa's office. Teresa answered. When she hung up, she said, "I'm going to go out front to talk to them, tell them to get lost. When you see me go through that door, you go down the

hall and out the back, okay? Susan Thomas is waiting there for you."

It sounded too easy, but it worked. When Teresa
went outside, the woman with the microphone and
the guy with the camera and a few other people
who I hadn't noticed before — reporters, I guess —
pressed in around her. I ducked down the hall. Mr.
Henderson was there, checking the locks on doors.

"You're late," he said.

I looked at him, but I didn't stop. I pushed my
way outside and there was Susan, in her car, just
outside the back door.

"Get down," she said after I climbed into the front
seat.

It seemed so stupid, having to hide like that, as if
I'd done something wrong — which I hadn't. But
then, I realized, neither had Riel. I ducked down
like Susan said and didn't pop up again until she
gave me the all-clear. I got ready to duck down
again when we got to Riel's street — just in case —
but she drove right by it.

"Hey," I said.

"We're going to my place," she said. "John doesn't
want anyone to bother you."

"Yeah, but — "

She looked at me and sort of shrugged. "It's what
he wants, Mike." Like that was it, there was no
point in discussing it or arguing about it.

Susan lived in a condo down by the water. One
entire wall of the place was glass and through it
you could look out over the harbour across to the

Island and, beyond that, clear across the lake. It was a big place, too, for one person — a huge living room, a pretty big dining room, a kitchen with an alcove to eat in and a walk-out to a balcony overlooking the water, a den where she kept her TV and her VCR, two big bedrooms, a couple of bathrooms, a laundry room. It was comfortable too. The place was nicely decorated and furnished and made you feel, once you got inside, that you could really settle there.

When we got inside, she dropped her purse on a table beside the front door and then picked up the phone. She must have called Riel because I heard her say, "He's fine," and "No, no one followed us." And that was it. He didn't ask to talk to me.

"You hungry?" Susan said.

I said I wasn't.

"You want something to drink?"

I shook my head. She went to the fridge, pulled out a bottle of white wine and poured herself a glass. She carried it to the couch in the living room and sat down.

"They didn't bother you too much, did they, Mike?"

I told her what the woman reporter had said. She shook her head.

"You wonder how someone like that would feel under the same circumstances," she said. "Personally, I don't think they think about it. When John was in the hospital that time, a couple of them practically camped out outside his door, waiting until they could pester him with their questions."

"Is that how you met him?" I said.

The question seemed to surprise her, but she nodded. "When you work in Emergency, you meet all kinds of people." She took a sip of her wine. "Did he tell you about what happened?"

I said he had.

"While he was in the hospital, I went up to see him a couple of times. He didn't talk much, though. He was kind of withdrawn, you know? Then he was discharged to a rehab place. And that was that, I didn't expect to ever see him again. Then one day I was down at U of T." The University of Toronto, she meant. "I'd been asked to talk to some medical students about emergency medicine. I was walking across campus, back to where I'd parked my car, and there he was, carrying a pile of books. A student. We talked and, well — " She shrugged, only this time she smiled. Then she said, "You want to watch a movie?"

I should have said no. Susan is a nice person and according to Riel she's a terrific doctor. But she's a woman. A woman who likes ballet. And the kind of novels that have the Oprah Book Club seal on the front. There were a few of them on a table near the TV. It turned out she also liked sad movies about messed up families where in the end they all say they love each other and everything turns out just fine. I tried to picture Riel watching one of those movies, and drew a blank. But then, I had trouble picturing him sitting beside her at the ballet, even though I knew he had gone with her.

The movie was pretty boring. Susan must have thought so too. Either that or she'd had a hard day, because about halfway through I heard a sound, like the world's smallest buzz-saw, and I looked over and saw her head tipped against the back of the couch. Her mouth was open. She was sound asleep and she was snoring. Great. I didn't want to switch off the movie in case she woke up and got offended. But I didn't want to have to sit there watching it, either, when it had already put her to sleep.

There were some magazines in neat piles on the shelf under her coffee table. I leaned over and grabbed a handful and flipped through them. Medical journals, gourmet cooking magazines and women's magazines. Well, what had I expected?

I waited for the movie to end. When she still didn't wake up, I picked up the remote and surfed until I found the hockey game. I watched that until the Leafs lost, then I found an action movie, which I watched by turning down the volume every time the actors turned up the firepower. Susan woke up about halfway through. She blinked at me. Her cheeks turned pink.

"I'm so sorry, Mike," she said. "That was rude of me."

I said it was no problem. I said if she was tired, she shouldn't let me keep her up. She told me where her guest room was and said that she had put out some fresh towels for me. I must have

looked surprised because then she said that Riel
was going to try to come by, but he didn't want any
reporters to show up at her place so he wasn't sure
when he was going to make it. She said if anyone
buzzed and she was asleep, I should check who it
was before letting them into the building.

"You sure I can't get you anything?" she said.

I told her I was fine.

I settled down on the couch again and watched
the end of the movie. When the news came on, I
switched to another channel and watched a re-run
of a cop show. I was thinking that maybe I should
get to bed when the buzzer sounded.

I waited a moment to see if Susan was going to
come out, but she didn't. So I went to the speaker
beside her door and pressed the button there and
asked who it was.

"Mike? That you?" Riel said. "Buzz me through."

Two minutes later he knocked on the door and I
let him in.

"What took you so long to get here?" I said.

He didn't answer my question. Instead he looked
around and said, "Where's Susan?"

"She went to bed a while ago," I said.

He seemed sort of disappointed, but he said,
"Sounds like a good idea. Get your stuff. Let's go."

On the way home he told me that Emily had
called and wanted me to call her back. "She said
it's about a wallet." He glanced at me. "Did you lose
your wallet, Mike?"

"No!" But, of course, that's what he would think:

irresponsible Mike. "You want to see it?"

He shook his head.

"Does Rebecca know about her?"

"Yeah," I said. Then, "It's not the same thing with Emily as it is with Rebecca."

"Oh."

I thought about telling Riel who she was, that she was Emily Corwin, but I didn't. I didn't see how it would help matters, but, boy, I sure saw how it might hurt him. It would just remind him of everything all over again, and I didn't want to do that. Besides, there was the whole thing with her stupid wallet. I had tossed the baggie and the wallet into a drawer. I hadn't even looked at it. Maybe I should have, though, because now I started to think that maybe the wallet wasn't the one with my fingerprints on it. Maybe it was similar, but not the same. That would be just like Emily. Except, geeze, she'd just had this news about her mother. You wouldn't think she would care about a stupid wallet. Well, maybe you would — if you knew her the way I did.

When we got home and into the house, I saw that Riel had a lot of papers spread out all over the dining room table. At first I thought they were papers he was grading. But then I saw photographs. I reached for one of them. He intercepted me.

"Bed," he said. "Now."

I watched him gather everything up and shove it all into a folder. Then he said, "I mean it, Mike."

CHAPTER TWELVE

It was quiet in the house when I woke up. Quiet and lighter than normal. I looked at the clock on my bedside table. Geeze — ten-thirty! I had missed first period, home form and the start of second period. Riel was gonna . . .

Riel.

How come Riel hadn't woken me up? The only thing I could think of: he was gone.

But he wasn't.

I raced downstairs and found him at the dining room table with all that stuff spread out again, the papers and the photographs. Also on the table, a bunch of empty beer bottles. Not a good sign. He didn't even look up when I came into the room.

"Is it a P.D. day," I said, "and nobody told me?"

His head swung up and he looked at me with bleary eyes. I wondered if he'd been to bed at all.

"It's ten-thirty," I said, and checked my watch. Correction. "Ten-forty-five."

"I'm taking the day off."

Another not-good sign. Riel could riff for an hour on the subject of duty and responsibility — how ninety percent of life was showing up, how when people depended on you, you should never let them down, how if you said you were going to do something, you should do it, no ifs, ands or buts. He could do another hour on the subject of punctuality — how people who were late for things were being disrespectful, how other people's time is valuable too, so you shouldn't leave them waiting around and wondering where you were, how tardiness betrays lack of maturity, lack of organization and lack of character.

But on a school day when he was supposed to be standing in front of a classroom, teaching, here he was sitting in his dining room staring through beer-soaked eyes at a table strewn with old information. He had no idea what time it was. He didn't even seem to be aware of the concept of time.

"Did you call them?"

"Huh?"

Boy, it was weird — me doing the parent thing, him looking blankly at me.

"Did you call the school?" I said.

He nodded. "I left a message." He peered down at his watch. "I left a message around seven. They'll get someone."

His cell phone rang. He stared down at it, like he was thinking over whether or not to answer it. Finally he picked it up and said hello. Then he said yeah, he was here. He said, fine. He put the phone down and said, "Get the door, will you, Mike?"

Huh?

The doorbell rang.

Detective Jones was standing on the porch. His expression was serious. He said hi without really looking at me. He wiped his boots on the mat when he came into the house, but he didn't take them off like he should have.

"I'm surprised to find you home on a school day, John," he said. He was taking it all in — the papers, the photographs, the empty beer bottles, Riel's bleary eyes, his hair that was standing up in places, probably from running his fingers through it while he read or thought or drank. Detective Jones reached down, put a finger on one of the photographs and spun it around.

"Where'd you get this stuff, John?"

Riel didn't answer.

"You think this is a good idea?" Detective Jones said.

"What's up, Dave?" Riel said.

Detective Jones looked at the photo again, but if you ask me, that wasn't what he was thinking about.

"Just checking to make sure you're okay."

"I'm fine." There was a snap to the words.

I backed up a little, out of their line of sight so there'd be less chance that one or the other of them would tell me to go upstairs or go to school.

Detective Jones pulled out a chair and sat down. "Maybe you should see someone," he said. "You know, make sure you're okay."

"Is that why you're here?" Riel said. "To see if maybe I need to pay a visit to my shrink?"

His *shrink*?

Detective Jones shook his head. "I'm here because you're my friend. Because I care what happens to you. Especially now."

"Meaning?" Another hard, tight delivery.

148

"Meaning it's not just you now, John. You've got the kid to think about."

He meant me. But neither of them turned to look at me. Neither of them shooed me away either.

They sat there across the table from each other for a moment. Then Detective Jones said, "We've identified the body."

Riel leaned forward.

"Gerard de la Rivière."

Riel leaned forward a little more. They stared at each other. Then Riel said, "Let me get this straight. The gun that was used to kill Tracie Howard was also used to kill de la Rivière. That's what you're saying?"

Detective Jones nodded.

Riel said, "You got a theory?"

"I got the only explanation I can think of that fits."

I wondered what the explanation was and inched forward so that I could see them both clearly.

Riel was shaking his head. "How does that make sense?"

How did *what* make sense?

"Tom Howard and Tracie aren't getting along," Detective Jones said. "Tracie has a big insurance policy and Tom is now the beneficiary. Tom gets the ball rolling, scares Tracie, freaks her out a little. But then maybe he doesn't want to do it himself — maybe he doesn't have the stomach for it, maybe he doesn't want to take the chance. So he hires de la Rivière to do it. Then, afterwards — " He shrugged.

Riel was still shaking his head.

"I've been through the file, John," Detective Jones said. "There doesn't seem to be anyone else who had a reason to want Tracie dead. And if it was de la Rivière on his own — if it was just a robbery that maybe went wrong — then how does he end up being killed with the same gun?"

"You found Howard yet?" Riel said.

"We're still looking for him." Detective Jones looked down at all the papers and pictures spread out on the table. "You remember anything from the case that might help? Anything that maybe didn't make it into a report — a gut feeling, a hunch, anything like that?"

"No."

Just like that, without even thinking it over.

Detective Jones pulled a couple of photographs closer and looked at them.

"We're going to keep de la Rivière's identity away from the media as long as we can. We'd like to find Howard first. Talk to him." He looked across the table at Riel. "We're going to take care of this, John. The best thing you can do is focus on what you have to do now — do your job, look after the kid, look after yourself. Okay?"

Riel didn't say anything.

Detective Jones stood up. "You think of anything or remember anything that could help us, give me a call. But you do your job and let us do ours. Okay?"

Riel said okay. He sounded like he meant it.

Maybe Detective Jones believed him and maybe he didn't. He said goodbye and headed for the door. He nodded at me to follow him, so I did, right out onto the porch. He closed the door behind me. "You okay, Mike?"

I nodded.

There were still a few reporters on the sidewalk, but at a glare from Detective Jones they backed up a couple of steps.

"You know how to get in touch with me, right, if anything comes up or if you just want to talk?" Talk about Riel, he meant. About how he was handling things.

I nodded again. When I went back inside, Riel was on his feet, gathering up all the papers, straightening them into a neat pile and putting them back into the thick file folder.

"You better get ready for school," he said. "I'll drop you."

"Where are you going?"

"I have some errands to run."

I looked at the empty beer bottles.

"*Now*, Mike," he said, irritated.

There were six empties on the table. They were just sitting there, not even on coasters, and if ever there was a guy who believed in coasters, it was Riel because, geeze, the last thing you wanted to do was leave rings on the finish of his brand new dining room table.

"Yeah? Is one of those errands a trip to the beer store?" I said. "Or maybe straight to a bar?"

That got his attention. He glanced at the empties and maybe, for a second, he looked embarrassed. Maybe.

"I'm legal," he said. "I don't need your permission to have a couple of beers."

I could see he was getting mad. Well, I was already there. I was so mad — and so scared — that I was shaking. "A *couple*?" I said.

"It's none of your business, Mike."

"Right," I said. "Have a beer or six or ten. Stop going to school. Get fired, why don't you? Children's Aid will love that."

He stared at me for what seemed like a long time. He looked at the beer bottles and frowned.

"There's somebody I have to see," he said.

I said, "Who?" and then waited for him to tell me that wasn't any of my business either.

Instead he said, "This guy de la Rivière — I used to know him. Professionally, I mean. He had a girl-friend. A dancer. Used to work in a bar." He glanced at me. "I need to talk to her."

"Shouldn't Detective Jones do that?" And there it was — just for a second, a little flash in his eyes. "Does he even know she exists?" I said.

"I heard she quit the business, got married and changed her name. I ran into her about a year ago — by chance. I hardly recognized her."

"So he *doesn't* know about her."

"He'll probably chase her down."

"But right now he doesn't know. He doesn't know her name either. Her new one, I mean."

"He's a good detective, Mike."

"As good as you?"

He got a surprised look on his face.

"You don't buy his theory, do you?" I said.

Nothing. He thought he was Mr. Inscrutable. He thought because he kept his face quiet, I had no idea what he was thinking. Maybe he thought I wasn't too smart. But I wasn't that dumb either.

"I want to go with you," I said.

"Forget it."

"Come on," I said. "School's half over. I'll stay out of the way. I promise." He was shaking his head at me, so I said, "Unless you're going some place you don't want me to know about."

CHAPTER THIRTEEN

We got into Riel's car and drove north until we left the city limits. We passed fields, a lot of them with signs planted in them that said either, "For Sale," or "Coming Soon," usually followed by the name of something that sounded like a cemetery, something like Pleasant Acres or Rolling Hills, but that really was the name of some new subdivision filled with gigantic houses that all look the same and have four-car garages because everyone in the family has to have a car to get around up there in the middle of what used to be farm country.

"When you said she worked in a hospital, I thought you meant someplace downtown," I said.

"You thought wrong."

No kidding. "How did you manage to run into her way up here?"

"I didn't. I ran into her downtown," Riel said. "She was at a medical seminar. I was there to pick up Susan."

"She quit being a dancer and became a doctor?"

"Nurse."

"And she told you where she works?"

"She didn't tell me much of anything," he said. "I don't think she would have told me her new name, but she was wearing a nametag. I think she was embarrassed, running into someone from her past like that."

"So how come you know where to find her now?"

Well, what do you know? The flicker of a smile.

"I took a look at the seminar sign-up sheet," he said.

"Once a cop, huh?"

He gave me a little more smile.

I wasn't sure why he had finally decided to let me come, what had made the difference. But I was glad to be there, mostly, I think, because of the way Riel looked now. Now that he knew something and now that he was doing something, he had perked up. He didn't look so much like a guy who was reliving one of the worst times of his life. Instead he looked like someone on a mission, someone who was determined to get the job done. Maybe it was a job he shouldn't have been doing, and maybe it wasn't going to turn out the way he wanted or expected, but at least it was something.

We finally pulled into a hospital parking lot.

"How do you even know she's going to be here?" I said.

Riel gave me a look. "I called ahead," he said. "Give me a little credit, huh, Mike? When I was working, I wasn't exactly Officer Stupid."

Right.

He opened the car door and got out. I stayed where I was until he ducked down, looked into the car, and said, "You coming or what?"

"You want me to?"

"Sure. You can make sure I don't get into the rubbing alcohol." It sounded like it was supposed to be a joke, but he didn't smile.

We went inside. Riel went up to the information desk and asked for directions. Then we walked up a flight of stairs and through a maze of hallways. I don't know how he did it, but he seemed to know exactly where he was going. Up ahead a woman in a pantsuit that looked like some kind of uniform turned around. When she saw Riel, she broke into a great big smile.

"John Riel," she said. "Is that really you?"

"Is that her?" I whispered to Riel.

He shook his head. "Kate," he said, and the two of them put their arms around each other and hugged. Then Kate pulled back a little.

"You look great," she said, giving him a pretty thorough once-over. "What brings you up here again?"

Again?

Riel told her he was looking for someone, then told Kate the woman's name. It turned out that Kate knew her — she said she'd just gone on her break and Riel could probably find her down in the coffee shop on the ground floor. Then Kate hugged Riel again and said how glad she was to see him and to see he was doing so well. She said, "Come back sometime. If I'm not mistaken, you still owe me a night on the town, from that bet you lost." He grinned — a real sparkly-eyed grin — and said he'd better do that because he didn't want her to think he was the kind of guy who welched on bets.

"Old girlfriend?" I said.

"Old nurse," he said. "I was here for a while. You

know, after. They do rehab work here. They've got a reputation for it."

Oh.

We went down to the coffee shop and stood just inside the door for a few moments while Riel scanned all the faces. Then he nudged me and nodded toward the back of the room. He started down between the tables to where a woman was sitting alone, smiling a little as she read and sipped coffee, enjoying her break. She was young and was also wearing a pantsuit that looked like a uniform, except that hers was a sort of peach colour whereas Kate's had been navy blue.

Riel said, "Paula?"

The woman was smiling when she started to look up, but when she saw it was Riel, she got a startled — no, a scared — look in her eyes. Then she straightened up and looked Riel over. Women were always looking him over. Especially pretty ones, and Paula sure was pretty. She had short blond-streaked hair and big blue eyes. I could see she was slim. She had been reading what looked like a textbook.

"Hello, Riel," she said. "You're looking good." She glanced at me and then back at Riel, a question in her eyes this time.

"My kid," he said. "Mike."

His kid? I wasn't the only one who was surprised by that. Paula looked at me again.

"Foster kid," Riel clarified.

She seemed impressed. I'm not sure why.

"You're looking good too, Paula. Nursing agrees with you, huh?"

"I love it," she said. "I'm good at it too."

Riel nodded. Then he said, "I need to talk to you, Paula. About Gerard."

Boy, did her face change fast. Away went the smile. In its place, a tight, serious mouth and a tight, serious look in her eyes. She glanced around, like she was afraid someone might have heard what he'd said. Riel pulled out a chair and sat down opposite her. I sat back a little.

"I haven't seen him in years," she said. "I'm out of that life now. I'm married. A guy I met while I was in nursing school. He doesn't know what I used to do for a living."

"I'm not here to make trouble for you, Paula. I just want to ask you a few things about Gerard."

"Why?" She sounded angry. Maybe bitter. "What kind of trouble has he got himself into now?"

"The worst kind there is," Riel said. "He's dead."

Her big blue eyes got even bigger.

"Dead?"

"When was the last time you saw him?" Riel said.

And even bigger. "You think *I* have something to do with him being dead?"

"No. And Paula? You can relax. I'm not a cop anymore."

She looked skeptical. "Private investigator?"

"School teacher."

She was so surprised that she laughed. It was a pretty sound. "You're kidding."

Riel shook his head. "Ask Mike."

She looked at me and I nodded. "He teaches history at my school," I said.

Her eyes went back to Riel and she looked at him like she was trying to picture him in a classroom, maybe chalk dust on his hands. Then her face got serious again. "Gerard's really dead?"

Riel nodded.

"What happened?"

So he told her. He said that Gerard de la Rivière was the person they'd found up in the woods in Caledon, maybe she'd read about it in the newspaper. She said she hadn't. She said she didn't like reading the newspaper, it was always depressing. She said she didn't watch TV news for the same reason. Riel talked softly when he told her that Gerard had been shot to death, and that it looked like it had happened a few years back. He didn't say anything about Tracie Howard, though, and he didn't tell her that Gerard had been killed with the same gun that had been used to kill Tracie Howard. I wondered why, but I didn't say anything.

"You remember when you saw him last?" Riel said.

She had been looking him straight in the eyes when he told her what had happened and I could see that she seemed sorry that de la Rivière was dead. Now she looked down at the textbook she had been reading.

"Paula?"

"Sure, I remember," she said. "I can't believe he's

dead." She shook her head. "I was eighteen years old when I met him. Right off the farm. No kidding. I'd never been in a place as big as Toronto. I was totally lost when I got off the bus. And then I met Gerard. We were together for four years." She shook her head again. "I think about those days, it's like I'm thinking about someone else's life, not mine, you know?"

Riel nodded.

"I never asked him what he was doing," she said. "I mean, I knew he was into some things that . . . " She shrugged. "I just never asked. I figured what I didn't know couldn't hurt me. He'd be there at the apartment with me and we'd have fun, and then he'd take off, be gone a few days, a few weeks, one time two months. He never said where he was going and I never asked." Her eyes met Riel's again, and she looked sorry. "Did he do something really bad?"

"Maybe," Riel said. "Now, about when you saw him last . . . "

She told him the exact day. "The reason I remember so well," she said, "it's my birthday. I thought that was going to be the day."

We both waited.

She smiled again, but looked sad when she was doing it. "I thought he was going to propose to me," she said. "You believe that?" Then, "Look at this place." We looked around at the cafeteria. It was big and bright and filled with people, a lot of them in white lab coats or pastel pantsuits like her own. "I

160

love it here. I feel like I belong here. I'm helping people and I like that. But back then? Back then I thought I'd have died and gone to heaven if Gerard had asked me to marry him. And when he showed me that ring, I thought, he must really love me. It was so big. So gorgeous. I have no idea how much a ring like that must have cost. I knew Gerard didn't have that kind of money — well, that he couldn't have got that kind of money legally. But I didn't care. I wanted that ring. He showed it to me and I waited for him to say the words. But he never did. He never proposed to me. He said I wouldn't believe how much that ring was worth to him, and then he said he had to go out. He put it in his pocket and left, and I never saw him again. He didn't even wish me happy birthday."

Riel thought about what she had said. "You never saw him again? Not even once?"

She shook her head.

"Did you ask around, find out where he might have gone?"

"I asked some guys he used to hang around with. They didn't know. To tell you the truth, I don't think they even cared. Not everybody felt about Gerard the way I did, and when I think about it now, I don't know why I felt that way."

"You didn't report him missing?"

She laughed. "To the cops? You kidding?"

"Paula, did you ever see him with anyone he might have been doing some work for?"

"If he was . . . *working* . . . for anyone, I didn't

want to know about it. Anyway, he didn't bring people like that around to the apartment."

"He never mentioned any names?"

"I told you, I didn't want to know what he was doing. I really didn't." She looked at Riel. "He could be very sweet. At least, he was to me."

"What about the ring?" Riel said. He asked her what she remembered about it — could she describe it? When he asked, I thought, a ring is a ring. Well, maybe it was to me, but not to Paula. It must have made a big impression on her, though, because she remembered it perfectly. She described the stone — a diamond that she said was blue, although I've never seen a diamond that didn't look clear, like ice. She even drew a little picture of the setting for Riel. He slipped it into his pocket and thanked her for her time.

"Are the cops going to show up and ask me the same questions?" she said. She looked nervous again.

"Probably," Riel said.

"And is it going to be in the papers and on TV?"

"Probably," Riel said. "Not right away, though. The police want to keep it quiet as long as possible. It gives them an edge while they try to figure out what happened."

"Because my husband . . . "

"You didn't do anything wrong," Riel said. He stood up and looked at her again. She'd been smiling when we first spotted her. She wasn't smiling now. "I'll see what I can do."

We were on our way out of the hospital when Riel said, "You go on ahead to the car. I have to make a phone call." He pulled his cell phone out of his pocket. I glanced around and saw a row of pay phones.

"Me, too," I said. "I'll meet you outside."

He went out while I fished for some coins in my pocket. I decided to return Emily's call before she left me another message and maybe told Riel even more about the mysterious wallet. I thought she would be in class so I'd just be able to leave a message, tell her when I'd be at the community centre so she could talk to me there instead of calling me at home. But she picked up on the second ring.

"My wallet," she said, as soon as she knew it was me. "I want it back."

Okay, so the one I took must have been the real deal — the one I had looked in, the one with my fingerprints on it. Otherwise why would she want it back?

"But you said — "

"There's something in it I need. Meet me tonight." Take-charge, rich girl Emily. Telling, not asking. Telling me when and where and, by the way, "Be there or I'll call the cops."

It was always a pleasure talking to Emily.

Riel was quiet on the way back to town.

"Did you tell him?" I asked after a while.

"Who?"

"Detective Jones. Dave."

No answer.

"You're not a cop anymore," I said.

Nothing. Well, okay. I looked out the window for a few kilometres. Looked and thought about Riel and his partner Marty and about what had happened. About Riel getting taken to emergency and, what do you know, meeting Susan. What some guys won't do. About Riel in rehab with pretty Kate — all the women he knew were pretty. About the girl he had shot. About Emily and her mother too. About Tom Howard, Emily's step-father, who Detective Jones thought had arranged to have Emily's mother killed. About — Wait a minute. Detective Jones thought maybe Tom Howard had hired someone to kill Tracie. But —

"Tom Howard didn't have an alibi," I said.

Riel glanced at me. He waited a moment before he said, "He had one. It just wasn't a good one."

That's what had been bothering Riel. Howard had said he was at a cabin. He had also said that no one had seen him there, no one could back up his alibi.

"*That*'s what you don't like, isn't it?" I said. "A guy hires someone to kill his wife so he can score a lot of insurance money and get all that jewellery to sell, and he doesn't establish an alibi for himself? An airtight alibi?"

He smiled. John Riel actually smiled. "Like I said, Mike. I wasn't exactly Officer Stupid."

* * *

After we left the hospital we went to a restaurant — a pretty good one — and had lunch. Then, on our way back to town, Riel said, what the heck, and we went to the movies. He didn't even ask me if I wanted to go. He just pulled off the highway at the nearest mall we came to and took me to the Cineplex and bought two tickets for an action picture that was just out, my kind of movie. For a while, I was really into it. Then I glanced at Riel and saw that although he was staring straight ahead, he wasn't really watching what was on the screen. He was chewing over the Tracie Howard case. I think he forgot I was even there. When the movie was over he said, "Not bad," like he'd been paying attention all the way through. I didn't call him on it. It was late in the afternoon by the time we got back home. When he got close to the house, he said, "Well, that's a nice change."

I took a look. Rebecca was sitting on the porch. Was that what Riel meant? It turned out it was — sort of.

"No press," he said. He stopped the car and got out. I scrambled out on my side.

Rebecca seemed flustered when she saw Riel. She gave me a panicky look. I guess she'd been hoping to catch me alone.

Riel went up the path first. He said hi to her. Her cheeks turned pink. She glanced at him and then looked down at the ground as she mumbled, "Hi, Mr. Riel."

Riel glanced over his shoulder at me, one eyebrow raised, maybe wondering if he'd done something wrong. I just shrugged. He kept on going, up the steps and into the house. Rebecca turned to make sure he was gone. Then she threw herself into my arms.

"I don't know why he makes me so nervous," she said. "I think because he used to be a cop. And because he always looks at me like he knows something, even when there's nothing to know."

He made me nervous too, sometimes, but I didn't tell her that. Instead I said, "What's up?"

"You weren't at school. I was worried." She glanced up at the house again. "Everyone's still talking about Mr. Riel, about what happened."

I shivered. The sun was dropping fast and, with it, the temperature. "You want to come inside?"

"No," she said, fast and loud, as if I had asked her if she wanted to be tortured or something.

"Geeze, Rebecca, he doesn't bite. He helped you out when you were scared about what happened to Robbie."

"I know. Hey, Mike? Why don't you come over to my place?"

I looked up at the house. Riel was in there, but I didn't know what he was doing.

"I can't," I said. "Not today. Anyway, I have to go into work early today."

She took my hand and held it for a moment. "Is everything going to be okay?"

I said yes because, at the time, I couldn't think of a single reason why it wouldn't be. Goes to show, huh?

CHAPTER FOURTEEN

Riel was at the dining room table when I went inside. He was going through the thick file folder again, the one that Detective Jones didn't think was such a good idea. But there were no beer bottles on the table in front of him.

"I've got a few things to do before work," I said, "so I'm going to take off, okay?"

"Sure," he said. He was thumbing through some papers. Then he looked up at me. "I'm sorry, what did you say?" I told him again. He glanced at his watch and nodded.

I ran up to my room and got Emily's wallet, which was still in the baggie. I shoved it into the pocket of my jacket and left the house.

* * *

When I found Neil, he was re-stocking the shelves in the Family section at Blockbuster. He was wearing a blue and yellow T-shirt tucked into chinos, and a name badge that said NEIL. He didn't look surprised to see me.

"I guess you heard," he said. "You know, about the body they found. They think it's related to what happened to Emily's mom."

I nodded.

"Have you seen her?" he said. "Is she okay?"

I shrugged. The longer I knew Emily, the more I got the feeling that she was someone who was hard to know, which is why I was at Blockbuster — to find out what Neil could tell me about her before I saw her for what I hoped would be the last time. To make sure it was the last time.

"To tell you the truth, Neil, I don't know how she is. She's hard to read, you know. How long did you go out with her, anyway?"

"Emily?" Now he looked surprised. "I never went out with her."

That threw me. "But I thought — "

He glanced around. "I'm supposed to be working."

"So show me the latest Bruce Willis movie," I said.

He made a face, but led me over to the Action section. "Okay," he said. "So I *wanted* to go out with her. Boy, did I ever. But she always said no. She has a new life now, that's what she said every time I asked her if maybe she wanted to go to a movie or something. She used to really like to say it and the worst thing was, she'd say it right in front of Sarah."

"You mean, her sister?"

He nodded. "I used to live just down the road from Emily and Sarah when their mother was still alive."

I remembered asking Emily about her sister the first time I was at her house. "Emily doesn't like to talk about her, huh?" I said.

He shook his head. "Sarah died last year."

"I know. She was paralysed, right?"

"A cop shot her."

"It was an accident," I said.

"Yeah," Neil said, bitter. "I bet that's what he says. But he shot her, severed her spinal cord. She was twelve years old. She spent the rest of her life in a home for people with chronic conditions. I was a year older than Emily when it happened. Afterward, I lost touch with her and Sarah. Their real dad suddenly showed up to claim them." He sounded even more bitter now. "He had no contact with them at all after the divorce. But the minute Emily's mother died, there he was. He packed them up and moved them out and I didn't see either of them again until about eighteen months ago. I needed to get my volunteer hours in, you know? So I volunteered to help at this long-term care place. It turned out to be the place where Sarah was."

He stopped and glanced up at the front of the store. I looked too. A guy behind the counter, a guy who wasn't wearing a blue and yellow T-shirt, which meant he was probably the manager, was staring at Neil. "Why don't we try this section?" Neil said in a voice that was loud enough to carry the whole length of the store. He steered me toward the Sci-Fi/Fantasy aisle.

"Sarah wasn't doing too well by the time I saw her again. People like her, people who can't move around, they get all kinds of health problems. I used to read to her. She really liked that. I read *Pride and Prejudice* to her, and then *Great Expectations*. Boy, that took forever. I think that's the longest book I ever read. That's how I ran into Emily again. She used to come and see Sarah. I never saw her dad." The look on his face said, *Thank God*. "But Emily was there every Wednesday afternoon like clockwork. Sarah said she came by on Sundays too."

"But her dad never visited?" I couldn't believe it.

"Sarah said he used to come pretty regularly for a while. But she said he had trouble handling the fact that she was paralysed."

He had trouble?

"She said he'd come and always sit in this one spot where she could hardly see him and he'd talk about how Emily was doing and what Emily was up to. She said he never asked her how she was doing. She said she knew he cared, but he was afraid, you know?" I didn't. "She said after about a year, he'd only show up every now and again. He'd get Emily to say he was busy, he couldn't get away — that kind of thing. She said after two years, he never came again."

"Nice guy."

"Sarah said she didn't care, but I could tell she did. She said she understood, but I knew she was hurt. But Emily always showed up and she always had something for Sarah — magazines, a book, something to eat. She used to do Sarah's hair for her too, and put mascara on her. She used to bring videos too, and books on tape so Sarah could listen all by herself. She liked to do that. Emily would do anything for Sarah, which I guess is why I fell for her. But then she'd go and say really insensitive things, like how she had a new life now with her dad and how she had put the past behind her, like she'd forgotten that Sarah couldn't do the same thing." He shook his head. "Sarah told me one time that she worried Emily was going to turn out just like her dad, caring about things more than about people."

I felt like saying that Sarah had it about right, but I didn't.

"Sarah was nine when her mother left her father. Emily was only four. Sarah said maybe that was why Emily acted like she did — she had no idea what it had been like between her parents. But Sarah remembered. She told me she used to hear them fighting. Then, after her mother started seeing Tom, her dad couldn't believe Sarah's mom was going out with a mechanic. She said the way he said *mechanic*, it sounded like garbage man or sewer worker."

To a guy like James Corwin, with his big house, his Jaguar, his library and his diamond stud, a mechanic probably *was* like a sewer worker, someone who was dirty all the time.

"She said when her father heard that her mother was going to marry Tom, he told her good luck raising a couple of kids on what a mechanic makes. She said he never called her or Emily, not even on Christmas or on their birthdays. Never. Not once. When Sarah's mom said she wanted sole custody, he went along with it. Didn't bother to contest it, is what Sarah said. She said she heard her mother tell Tom, he's just waiting for us to fall flat on our faces, he's waiting until one of the kids needs braces and we can't afford them or until they're old enough to go to university and we can't pay for it, he's waiting for me to ask him for something, anything, so he can tell me, I told you so."

"Nice guy," I said.

"The whole time her mother was divorced, Sarah's father talked to Sarah exactly once," Neil said. "He called her after her mother married Tom Howard. Sarah's mother was going to change Sarah and Emily's names legally to Howard. She had to notify Sarah's dad. He called Sarah and asked her if that was what she really wanted."

"Why wouldn't she?"

"Her dad told her, you're a Corwin. Once a Corwin, always a Corwin."

"And?"

"And nothing. A couple of weeks later, Sarah and Emily's mother was killed. And a few months after that, that cop shot Sarah and I never saw her or Emily again until I started volunteering at the long-term care place."

* * *

When I left Blockbuster, I thought I was going to be late. But I wasn't. I got to the restaurant before Emily did. I slipped into a booth near the window that gave me a good view of the door and an even better one of the community centre, and ordered a Coke. Then I thought, wait a minute. I pulled out the baggie and shook the wallet out onto the table. I took a paper napkin from the dispenser on the table and carefully wiped the wallet all over. That was how they did it on TV, right? A guy leaves fingerprints at the scene of the crime, so he takes a rag or a cloth and wipes them away. I wiped the wallet all over on the outside, then I opened it up — because I had opened it up that time too — and I wiped all over the inside. I tried to remember what I had touched. The outside and the inside of the wallet. Also, her student card and her transit pass. I checked, but those weren't in the wallet now. She must have taken them out before she bagged it because, of course, she needed those and they would have been a hassle to replace. She didn't strike me as the kind of girl who liked a hassle, even when she was blackmailing someone.

I had checked the money compartment that time too, so I checked it again now. The money was still in there — if there was something she had plenty of, hassle-free, it was money. I wiped the inside of that compartment and then wondered if they could pull fingerprints off money. Probably they could. But there would be lots of other prints on the bills too, so probably it wasn't a big deal. At least, I hoped it wasn't.

I hadn't touched anything else, so I gave the whole wallet another wipe. And then I remembered what she had said: she wanted the wallet back because there was something in it she needed. But what? There was nothing in there except money. What was she up to? Maybe she just wanted the wallet back, so she could have something on me again. She seemed to like that. Or maybe I was wrong about the money. Maybe she did need it. Maybe her daddy gave her an allowance — here's what you get and you don't get any more. Then I remembered her room and all the stuff — expensive stuff — that was in it, and I decided, no, that couldn't be it.

I opened the wallet again, still holding it in the napkin — I'd learned my lesson. There was one compartment I hadn't looked in. A little zippered compartment. I unzipped it.

There was something inside. Something folded up that looked like it had been cut out of the newspaper. I pulled it out — it had been folded over and over, too many times, and had been kept folded for too long. I unfolded it carefully. The paper was yellowish and brittle, and coming apart along a few of the fold lines.

It was a newspaper article about Emily's mother, the investigation of her murder, and the arrest of Thomas William Howard. Included with the article was a picture of Tom Howard — a nice, average-looking guy with the kind of face you see almost anywhere. Tom Howard, who had shot Riel after Riel shot his step-daughter. Tom Howard, who had been acquitted in the end because the Crown hadn't been able to convince the jury beyond a reasonable doubt that he had killed his wife. Tom Howard, who had got all that insurance money but never had a chance to enjoy it because of all his legal fees. I looked at the photo, yellowed with age.

If he really hadn't done it, boy, he'd sure been through the grinder for nothing. And if he *had* done it, well, he'd got away with it.

"What is it with you?" Emily said, startling me, making me jump. I'd had a good view of the door, but I hadn't been looking at it. She snatched the wallet out of my hand and then grabbed the newspaper clipping. "Who said you could go through my wallet — again?"

"Is that what you needed?" I said, nodding at the clipping.

She stared down at it.

"You think he did it?" I said.

Her head came up and she gave me a cold look. "What do you know about it?"

More than you think, Emily. Hey, I live with the guy who shot your sister, the guy your step-father shot. Boy, what *don't* I know?

"It's just a question," I said. "I mean, he's your step-father, right?"

"He's nothing to me. I have a father. And you know what? I'm glad they sent me back to live with him after Tom was arrested. And I'm sorry my mother ever married Tom Howard."

"I heard your dad never contacted you once after your mother left him."

She didn't like that. It was okay for her to know stuff about me, but she didn't like that I knew stuff about her.

"Who told you that?" she said.

I just shrugged.

"He told me he was sorry," she said. "He said he was so mad at my mother that it blinded him. He said he wished now that he hadn't given up custody. He said maybe things would have turned out differently. He says, who knows, maybe my sister wouldn't have . . . maybe she never would have found . . . " Her expression was fierce. "It just might have been different, that's all."

"I'm sorry about what happened. With your mom, I mean. And your sister."

She still looked angry, but she said, "I guess you know what it feels like." She sat down opposite me and stared at the clipping for a long time, reading it, I think. Then she smoothed it out, refolded it and tucked it back into her wallet. "I found it in Sarah's things," she said, "after she" — she hesitated — "after she died." She looked directly at me, as if she were daring me to say something or to ask her something about her sister. When I didn't, she slipped her wallet into her backpack. Then she leaned against the upholstered back of the booth. "So," she said, "Why don't you introduce me to that creepy guy you say is so interested in me."

"What?" Why did she care about that, especially now? Or maybe that was the reason — Mr. Henderson gave her something to think about, something other than her mother and her sister. "You want to meet Mr. Henderson?"

"Why not? He seems to be dying to meet me. And you're working tonight, aren't you?"

"Yeah, but — "

"Great," she said. "Let's go."

She was out of the booth and at the door before I fished out the money to pay for my Coke. By the time I caught up with her, she was across the street and striding toward the community centre.

"Hey!" I said. I grabbed her by the arm. She whirled around and smiled at me. "Hey, what if he's some creepy stalker guy?" I said.

"He's not going to do anything to me now," she said. "There are people in there. And you'll be with me."

"Me?" I wasn't sure I wanted to be around when Emily pulled her superior act on someone else, especially a guy like Mr. Henderson who, let's face it, was pretty pathetic even if he was weird.

She grabbed me by the hand and hauled me inside. Teresa Rego was out in the main hall, tacking something to a bulletin board. She turned and looked at us.

"Everything okay, Mike?"

I nodded.

"Excuse me," Emily said, flashing her pretty white rich-girl smile. "But have you seen Mr. Henderson?"

Teresa looked upset, I wasn't sure why. "If he's still here, he's probably downstairs."

"*If?*" I said.

"He just informed me that he quit. He's leaving, with exactly no notice."

Emily pulled me toward the stairs before I could say anything.

"I don't think this is such a good idea," I said.

"You're not scared, are you?"

"No. But what's the point?"

She stopped on a landing and turned to me. "The point is, I don't like some old guy taking an interest in me." She pulled me down the stairs and through the door to the basement.

The basement was huge. Part of it was activity rooms. The pottery workshop was down there. So was a room that was painted black and was used mainly by drama groups. They could make a lot of noise down there and no one heard them. But most of the basement was storage rooms and the boiler room, places like that. We found Mr. Henderson outside the boiler room — a big windowless place with a metal door. He had his back to us. A sports duffle bag sat on the floor at his feet. He was locking the door or unlocking it, I couldn't tell which.

"Is that him?" Emily whispered to me. I nodded. "Hey!" she called. "Hey, you, Mr. Henderson."

He turned slowly, twisting in a way that wouldn't put too much pressure on his bad leg. He looked at Emily and his face went slack, like he couldn't believe what he was seeing, like he wasn't sure he wanted to believe it.

"Hey, I hear you want to meet me," she said, all rich-girl snotty now. "Well, here I am."

Mr. Henderson said, "Emily."

Just that — one word, her name — and the sassy expression vanished from her face. She peered at him and shook her head.

"I've been trying to find you," he said. "And when

I saw you here . . . " He bowed his head. "I was afraid to talk to you. And then you vanished again and I couldn't find you. Jim's not listed. And no one would tell me where he lived. I was going to go to your school, but . . . "

"You two know each other?" I said.

Emily was staring at him, her mouth hanging open, like she was in shock. She kept staring at him, but she said to me, "He killed my mother."

I looked at Mr. Henderson again and, in my mind, I compared him to the faded picture I had seen in the newspaper clipping in Emily's wallet. It wasn't the same person at all.

"Emily, this is Mr. Henderson."

"He's Tom *Howard*," she said, her eyes still firm on him. "He's Tom Howard and he murdered my mother and got away with it. But he's not going to get away this time. The police are looking for you, Tom. They found the other body."

"Emily," Mr. Henderson said. Just the one word again. A name and a prayer.

"Murderer," she said, her voice loud and shrill. "Murderer."

She turned to look at me. "Go and find someone. Tell them to call the cops."

"Geeze, Emily — " I still couldn't believe it. But she seemed so sure, and he wasn't denying it. And now that it was all over the news that the police were looking for Tom Howard, Mr. Henderson had quit his job. He hadn't even given notice. Was he running away?

I heard something behind me, near the stairs. I saw Emily's expression change when she turned toward the sound. She started to move back in that direction, away from Mr. Henderson.

"Emily," he said again. "I didn't do it."

But she kept right on going. She never looked back. And as Mr. Henderson watched her go, the expression on his face changed too, from soft and kind of sad to something harder and colder. What was going on? As I turned to look, I caught a glimpse of Mr. Henderson out of the corner of my eye — he ducked down, unzipped his duffle bag and rooted around in it. At the end of the hall near the stairs, I saw Detective Jones. Teresa Rego was with him. She was pointing at Mr. Henderson. Detective Jones said something to her and she nodded. She stayed where she was. He came toward us, holding out his badge and ID.

"Thomas Henderson," he said. "Police."

Mr. Henderson straightened up slowly. He murmured something — it sounded like "Sorry" — and then grabbed hold of my arm. That's when I saw what he had taken out of the duffle bag. It was a gun. You see a gun on TV or in a movie and it looks like no big deal. But when you see them on cops' belts — which I have, several times — the first thing you notice is that they're bigger and scarier than they look on the little screen or even the big one.

Detective Jones saw the gun too. "Hey now," he said, sounding like a driving instructor or a judge at a flower show, he was that calm. But his eyes flitted from the gun to Mr. Henderson's face and back again, like maybe he was trying to figure out if Mr. Henderson was going to use it and, if he was, when. And who exactly he was planning to shoot. "Hey, Tom . . . Is it okay if I call you Tom? I just want to talk to you, that's all."

I noticed more movement somewhere behind Detective Jones. It was Detective London, way down at the end of the hall. Detective Jones must have caught the look in my eyes because he glanced back over his shoulder.

Mr. Henderson tightened his grip on me. "Get rid of your gun and tell him" — Detective London, he meant — "to get rid of his," he said to Detective Jones. "If either of you tries anything, I'll shoot this kid."

Me. He meant me.

Detective Jones studied Mr. Henderson for a moment. He said, "Tom, all we want to do is talk to you. Why don't we keep it that way, okay? Put that thing away and we won't have to — "

"Now," Mr. Henderson said. He didn't shout. He didn't even raise his voice. But you could tell that he meant business. At least, I could. "Tell him you're going to count to three," he said. He meant Detective London. "Tell him when you get there, you're both going to take out your guns with your left hands. Tell him you're both going to unload your guns and then you're going to slide them down here. You got that?" He pressed the barrel of his own gun into my neck so hard that I couldn't help it, I let out a little yowl.

Detective Jones asked me if I was okay. I said I was. Then he called back over his shoulder to Detective London, telling him exactly what Mr. Henderson had said. He made sure Detective London knew about the gun that was digging into me and I was grateful for that. I was also grateful that Detective Jones was standing in front of me instead of Detective London. I wasn't sure Detective London would have been so careful to make sure I was all right. I could see from the look on his face, small as it was way down the hall, that he wasn't thrilled about what was going on. But when Detective Jones got to three, I saw him pull out his gun, just like Detective Jones was doing, and unload it. Detective Jones watched me the whole time. I was sweating hard and it was a good thing Mr. Henderson had such a tight grip on me because my knees were buckling.

After his gun was unloaded, Detective Jones set it down carefully and slid it toward me. I felt it hit the toe of my left sneaker. Then I heard a skittering sound — metal on concrete — and Detective London's gun slid down the corridor past Detective Jones.

"Kick them back to me," Mr. Henderson said to me.

I did and then he kicked them back behind him, into the boiler room. I heard them skid across the floor inside. After that, we all stood there. No one moved. I wondered what was going to happen next. What was he going to do?

182

I saw Emily halfway down the hall between the two detectives. She was pressed up against the wall like she was trying to make herself as flat as paper in case anyone started shooting.

"Okay," Detective Jones said. He was looking hard at Mr. Henderson. "Okay, Tom. Now what do you want to do? You want to put that thing away so we can talk?"

Mr. Henderson didn't want to do that. We all waited. Then Mr. Henderson said that what he wanted was Riel.

"Get him here," he said. "You've got thirty minutes."

He jerked me backward, through the boiler room door, into blackness. The door clanged shut. His fingers bit hard into my arm as he said, "Lock it."

"What?"

"Lock it."

It sounded like the end of the world when the deadbolt *tchonked* into place.

"The light," he said.

"Huh?"

"Next to the door. The light."

I felt around until I found the switch. A light came on overhead. I looked over at the door. It was heavy and metal and, as far as I could tell, it was the only way out.

Mr. Henderson jerked me deeper into the room, away from the door.

"Turn around," he said. "Put your hands on the wall."

I did what he said. I did everything he said. I put my hands flat against the wall where he could see them. I put my feet together and kept them together while he wrapped duct tape around them. I put my hands behind my back and let him tape my wrists together too. Then I squirmed around to face him when he told me to and I sat down on the floor as best I could. Now what, I wondered. Maybe he read my mind. He said, "Now we wait."

CHAPTER FIFTEEN

Thirty minutes. The time it takes to watch a sitcom on TV. A little less than half of a math class. Time that could zip by or creep by.

Mr. Henderson stood close to the door the whole time we waited, so that he could hear what was going on outside. He made me sit beside him so that he could watch me, not that I was going anywhere. If the duct tape people ever needed someone to go on TV and say how strong their product was, I was their man. I couldn't even move my wrists, let alone work them free.

After a little while, I asked him how come he wanted to see Riel. He didn't answer. I told him, "He's not a cop anymore," and he looked surprised, so I guess he hadn't known that. It didn't seem to change his mind, though. He stayed where he was, in front of the door, and waited.

I heard them even before I saw Mr. Henderson straighten — voices in the hallway on the other side of the metal door. But they were muffled, so I couldn't make out at first what they were saying. Mr. Henderson pressed his ear to the door. His eyes were tight and focused on something I couldn't see. Then I heard a voice, loud and clear. Detective Jones.

"Tom? John Riel is here."

Then Riel identified himself so that Mr. Henderson would know that he was really there.

Mr. Henderson stepped back from the door a pace. He reached down and grabbed the front of my jacket.

"Get up," he said.

He hauled me to my feet and pulled me over in front of the door. I had to sort of hop sideways to get there. He didn't hurry me and he didn't get mad at me when I stumbled and he had to strain to keep me on my feet.

"Tom?" It was Riel's voice again. "Tom, I need to know that Mike is okay."

Mr. Henderson nudged me. He told me to answer Riel. I called out through the door that I was fine, that Mr. Henderson hadn't hurt me.

"Okay, Tom," Detective Jones said. "It's good that the boy is okay. No one is hurt. That's good. If you open the door, Tom, and let the boy out, we can work things out."

"I want him to come in," Mr. Henderson said. "I want John Riel to come in."

For a moment there was complete silence on the other side of the door. Then I heard a hissing sound, like people whispering.

"We'll have to get permission for that, Tom," Detective Jones said. His voice sounded strained now. "John Riel isn't a police officer anymore. We have policies that we're supposed to follow. You understand that, right, Tom?"

Mr. Henderson had one hand clamped around my arm. In the other, he held the gun.

"You have one minute," he said, his voice sounding calm and clear. "John Riel comes in here or I won't be able to guarantee the boy's safety."

I felt myself go cold all over.

"I hear you," Detective Jones said. "We want to do everything we can to make this work, Tom. But it's going to take us a little longer than one minute — "

"Forty-five seconds," Mr. Henderson said.

"Tom, I understand what you're saying but — "

"I'll come in," Riel said.

Someone — Detective Jones, I think — said something that I couldn't make out. Then I heard Riel's voice. He said he was going in and that was that. Then he said to Mr. Henderson that he was ready.

Mr. Henderson made me stand right in front of him. He reached around me and unlocked the door. He pressed the gun into my ear, hard, and said to Riel that he could come in now, but he'd better come in alone or else.

I held my breath. The door inched open and then there was Riel in the opening. I saw Detective Jones behind him and, farther back, Detective London and some other cops in uniform.

"Inside," Mr. Henderson said. "Now." He jammed the gun harder into my ear. I kept my mouth shut, but my eyes started to water. Geeze, I didn't want Riel to think I was crying.

Riel pushed the door shut.

"Lock it," Mr. Henderson said.

I heard the deadbolt slide into place. Mr. Henderson dragged me back from the door, keeping me in front of him, between him and Riel.

Riel turned around slowly, his hands up so that Mr. Henderson could see that he wasn't armed. When he was finally facing us, he looked at me, not Mr. Henderson.

"You okay, Mike?" he said.

I nodded. My ear hurt. My knees felt wobbly. But, yeah, I was okay. So far.

Riel looked me over, like he wanted to see for himself. Then he looked past me, at Mr. Henderson.

"I don't know what you want, Tom," he said. "But I do know that it has nothing to do with this boy. You want a hostage, fine. I'll be your hostage. But let the boy go."

Mr. Henderson didn't loosen his grip; he tightened it. "You shot Sarah. She was like a daughter to me and you shot her and now she's dead," he said. He jammed the gun harder against my ear and, I couldn't help it, I let out a yelp. Riel jumped a little. "You shot Sarah," Mr. Henderson said again.

Riel stared at him. He had that look in his eyes, the same one he'd had the night he told me about what had happened — like a guy who had just been jolted awake from what he thought was a bad dream only to find out that it hadn't been a dream after all.

"I'm sorry about Sarah," Riel said. Something in his eyes told me — told me for sure — that he was seeing what he had done, and that all the years since it had happened hadn't faded the memory. If

188

anything, time had just sharpened it.

"Mike's just a kid, Tom," he said. "He didn't have anything to do with it."

Then I was falling.

It probably took me a second or two to realize what was happening and everything that happened after that probably took another few seconds. I was falling because Mr. Henderson had shoved me hard to one side and with my ankles and hands taped, there was nothing I could do to keep myself upright. I was dropping fast toward a concrete floor and while I fell, I looked back at Mr. Henderson and saw his hand with the gun swing so that it was pointing directly at Riel. Then I hit. My elbow made contact first, followed by the rest of my body. It hurt so bad that my eyes teared up. But I forced myself to twist around and saw Mr. Henderson pointing his gun at Riel. I don't know what I expected Riel to do, but I sure didn't expect him to lower his hands and then to hold them away from his body the way he did, like he was saying, Okay then, go ahead, shoot, if that's what you want.

Except that Mr. Henderson didn't shoot. He stepped toward Riel, holding the gun out in front of him. At first I thought, he wants to get really close, boy, he wants to make one hundred percent sure that he doesn't miss when he shoots the guy who shot his step-daughter.

But nothing happened. Mr. Henderson didn't shoot and Riel didn't move, except for his eyes, which shifted to Mr. Henderson. He looked at him and I could see he was still remembering. His hands were down and he sort of shrugged. Then he tipped his head back a little and it hit me: he wants it to happen. I glanced at Mr. Henderson, who was closer to Riel now, so close that if Riel wanted to, he could reach out and grab the gun from Mr. Henderson's hand. And I thought, Mr. Henderson wants it to happen too. He's the same as Riel. But Riel still didn't move. Then Mr. Henderson turned the gun on me. I saw his finger move, the one that was on the trigger. That's when I said, "No."

I don't know if that's what made Riel act, but he did. He stepped closer to Mr. Henderson and put his hand on the barrel of the gun and pulled it around so that it wasn't facing me anymore, it was facing him. And I said, "No! It wasn't your fault!"

They stood there for what seemed like an hour, but it was probably only a couple of seconds. Mr. Henderson was holding the gun by its grip, his finger still on the trigger, and Riel was holding it by the barrel, which was pointed directly at him. Mr. Henderson seemed to be waiting for something. Waiting for Riel to turn the tables on him, I realized. Riel was waiting too. So I said it again. "It wasn't your fault, John." When he still didn't move, I said, "Please."

Riel looked at me. He shook his head as if he were finally waking up. He was still holding onto the gun barrel. He put his other hand on Mr. Henderson's hand. He said, "Listen to me, Tom. I know you didn't kill Tracie." He told Mr. Henderson about the body that had been found in the woods in Caledon, and about the bullet that had been found there too. Told him that the guy had been killed with the same gun that had killed Tracie. He said he knew Mr. Henderson hadn't done it because the guy who had been killed had been seen with Tracie's ring just before he disappeared. The guy went to meet someone and never came back.

"When that happened," Riel said, "when that guy disappeared — when he was killed — you were in detention, Tom. You understand what I'm saying? I know it wasn't you. It couldn't have been."

Mr. Henderson hadn't let go of the gun. Riel kept looking at him. His eyes never left Mr. Henderson. Then he said, "Tom" — that's all, just his name — and Mr. Henderson relaxed his grip on the gun. I figured he was going to let Riel take it, so I started to relax too. My elbow was throbbing. When I rolled over to sit up, it hurt so bad that I groaned. Riel glanced at me. He still had his hand on the gun barrel, but he looked relaxed too. Then he startled when Mr. Henderson wrenched the gun out of his hand and turned it on himself. I saw Riel move, but — *BLAM!* — the sound almost deafened me.

CHAPTER SIXTEEN

I don't know exactly what the cops and whoever else outside the door were doing, but I do know what it sounded like they were doing — going nuts. Someone hammered on the door. Someone — Detective Jones — shouted, "What's going on in there?" He called Riel's name and mine. Riel called back that everything was fine. He had Mr. Henderson's gun in his hand. Mr. Henderson was on the floor where Riel had knocked him. He looked dazed lying there, rubbing his sore leg and staring up at Riel. Riel took the bullets out of the gun and put them in his pocket.

"You okay?" he said to me.

I nodded. My elbow hurt so bad I could hardly bend it, but, yeah, I was okay. Mostly I was relieved. For a while there I'd been pretty sure that Mr. Henderson was going to shoot Riel — and I'd been pretty sure that Riel was going to let him, right up until Mr. Henderson had turned the gun on me. And then I'd been pretty sure that Mr. Henderson wanted Riel to take the gun and shoot him.

Riel unlocked the door and the place filled up fast with cops. A couple of them got hold of Mr. Henderson and put handcuffs on him. Riel got a pocketknife from Detective Jones, then kneeled down beside me and sliced through the duct tape around my wrists and ankles. After I peeled off the tape, he helped me to my feet.

"You sure you're okay?" he said.

I nodded, even though my elbow was throbbing. I looked over at Mr. Henderson. He was on his feet now too, with a cop on either side of him, holding onto him. Riel went over to Detective Jones, and then they both retreated to a corner of the room to talk. Riel seemed to be trying to make a point, but Detective Jones kept shaking his head. Right after the cops took Mr. Henderson away, Riel came back to me and took me by the arm to guide me out of the room. I thought we were going home, but we didn't, not right away. Instead, Riel took me up to Teresa Rego's office and made me sit down. He got me some water and made me drink it. Then he sat down and we waited for Detective Jones, who showed up after a few minutes and got me to tell him everything that had happened before he showed up and while I was inside the room with Mr. Henderson.

Mostly I told him the truth. What I mean is, everything I said was true, I just didn't say everything that happened. For sure I didn't tell him how scary it had been, how I'd been sure they both wanted it. The reason I didn't is because it hadn't turned out that way, so I figured that it didn't matter. Not enough to tell the cops, anyway.

After I finished talking and Detective Jones finished writing down what I said, we went out to Riel's car. Detective Jones got into his car to follow us home. I slid into the front seat of Riel's car and, just like that, I started shaking all over. I couldn't stop. Riel noticed. He reached over and zipped up my parka for me, then took off his scarf and wound it around my neck.

I was still shaking when Riel got out of the car and stood on the curb, waiting for me. I got out and followed him up to the house. Detective Jones arrived right after us. Susan was already there. She opened the door and stood aside to let us into the front hall. For a couple of seconds she hung there, looking at Riel. Then she stepped in close to him and put her arms around his waist. He pulled her closer and held her. Her head rested against his chest and they stood like that for a minute. Then she turned and looked at me and said, "Are you okay, Mike?"

I nodded, but I was still shaking.

Riel said, "He hurt his arm."

Susan insisted on taking a look. She made me bend it and straighten it out. Then she said, "Nothing's broken, but it's going to hurt for a while. And you'll probably have a nasty bruise." She looked at Riel. "I made sandwiches," she said. "And coffee."

We all followed her into the kitchen and sat down. I took half a sandwich and ate it in about two seconds. I hadn't realized how hungry I was. I ate a couple more right after that. Riel and Susan went into the other room. I heard them talking in soft voices. Detective Jones took a sandwich and then excused himself to make a phone call, which left me alone at the kitchen table.

Riel's file folder lay on the table. It was thick with papers and photographs. I pulled out one of the photos. It was the same one I had seen in Emily's room — Emily, Sarah and their mother. I flipped open the file folder and then wished I hadn't. The other photos weren't nearly as warm and cheerful as the first one. They were photos of Emily's mother — *after*.

I flipped them over and looked at the papers instead — a couple of police reports, it looked like — and the newspaper and magazine clippings. There were lots of them, about the murder of Tracie Howard, about what had happened to Sarah, about Riel, about Riel's partner who had been killed. Then about the trial. A lot of the articles included pictures — pictures of Tracie, of Tom Howard. Of Tracie and James Corwin on their wedding day — Tracie in a wedding dress, James in a tux. Tracie and James with the two little girls, James with his arms around them, holding them all in close to him, looking pleased that they were *his* daughters.

"One big happy family, huh?" said a voice behind me. Detective Jones.

"Except she's not smiling," I said. I meant Tracie.

Detective Jones sat down at the table and reached for another sandwich. "As I recall from the file, she left him not long after that one was taken." He flipped the picture over. There was a date on the back. "Yeah. She was out of that marriage about a year later."

"Because she'd met Tom Howard?" It seemed

funny to be calling him that when all this time I had known him as Mr. Henderson.

Detective Jones shook his head. "That's the way James Corwin saw it. According to Tom Howard, he and Tracie knew each other, but that wasn't the reason she left James. She just wanted out of the marriage. She took the girls, moved out, and went back to work."

"Back to *work*? But James Corwin is loaded. She must have got money from him, from the divorce. And child support."

Detective Jones shrugged. "What can I say? She signed a pre-nup. When she left him, all she got was a hundred grand. And the kids. She had an insurance policy she paid for herself in case anything happened to her, probably because James gave her a hard time about child support. He was always late making the payments. She had to get a lawyer after him. He just didn't care. And this was a guy who was worth millions. He's worth more now." He shook his head. "That says something about Tracie and James's marriage. You have to *really* not like a person to turn your back on that kind of money."

Riel came into the room and sat down at the table. He looked tired.

"Where's Susan?" I said.

"She had to get back to the hospital." He picked up a sandwich, but didn't even take a bite of it. "Tom couldn't have killed de la Rivière," he said. "He was in detention when de la Rivière disappeared. He never made bail. There's no way he could have done it."

Detective Jones didn't look happy. "Geeze, John," he said, "it's bad enough you went into that room. You know how much grief I'm going to get for that? But going off by yourself to see de la Rivière's girlfriend — "

Riel looked surprised.

"Yeah, I found out about that, John." He shook his head. "You're a teacher now, not a cop. Remember?"

Maybe he didn't because he said, "Tom killing her — that made some kind of sense. The guy's got a temper. He gets angry, lashes out at his wife and kills her without thinking. Then realizes he doesn't have much of an alibi, so he does the best he can to point the finger at someone else. He doesn't do a good job of it, but, hey, he didn't mean to do it. That made sense. But a guy who hires someone to kill his wife? That's planning. And if you're planning it, if you're going to hire someone to do it, you're absolutely going to have an alibi and it's going to be airtight. You're going to have solid witnesses who can swear where you were at the time it happened." He kept his eyes steady on Detective Jones. "You see what I'm saying, Dave?"

"You're thinking the husband," Detective Jones said. "The first one. James Corwin. You know where he was when it happened?"

"At a political fundraiser," Riel said. "A gala. With over five hundred of the most influential people in the country."

Detective Jones sighed. Riel got up and went to the fridge.

"You want something to drink?" he said.

"I'll take a pop," Detective Jones said.

"Me too," I said.

Riel stood with the fridge door open. I waited. When he swung the fridge door shut, he had three cans of pop in his hand. He looked at me. I gave him a little smile. Inside, I felt a big one.

"What about motive?" Detective Jones said. "Tracie and James had been divorced for three years. He gave up any claim to the kids. Never even tried for custody. As far as I've been able to tell, he had no contact with Tracie or the kids. Put that together with a blue-chip alibi and you get nothing."

Riel handed the cans of pop around.

"Yeah, I know," he said. "That's why we never went after him. He was out of it."

"He called Sarah," I said.

They both turned — Riel to the left, Detective Jones to the right — and stared at me.

"More," Riel said.

"The whole time Tracie was with Tom Howard, Sarah and Emily's father never contacted them, not even on their birthdays or at Christmas," I said. "But he called Sarah a couple of weeks before Tracie was shot. Tracie was going to change Emily and Sarah's names legally from Corwin to Howard."

Riel stared at me. Detective Jones said, "How do you know this, Mike?"

I told them about meeting Neil and what he had said to me. Riel looked at me.

"The Emily you know from the community centre is Emily *Corwin*?" he said.

I nodded.

"But you never told me it was the same girl."

I glanced at Detective Jones, who shrugged and looked at Riel.

"Oh," Riel said, the tone of his voice and the look on his face telling me that I didn't have to explain. Except that I knew I would, eventually, because I'd kept quiet not for the reason he thought, not only because I wanted to save his feelings, but because I wanted to save myself.

For a while nobody said anything. Detective Jones took a swallow of pop. Riel looked down at the table. I looked down at the picture again. Tracie Howard — no, she was Tracie Corwin then — standing next to and a little in front of her husband James. Her left hand rested on Sarah's shoulder. Something glinted on it. Her ring. Her diamond ring, the one that had been taken when she was killed. One of James's hands was around Tracie's waist. The other one was on Emily's shoulder.

I looked at that photograph. Then I pulled out the one of Tracie and James on their wedding day. I looked at newspaper pictures of him too, from the press conferences later, after Tracie had been killed, after Sarah had been shot, when he was attacking the police for incompetence. I looked at them one by one while Detective Jones chewed on a sandwich and Riel sipped his ginger ale. When I flipped back to the photograph of James and Tracie Corwin and the two kids, I became aware that Detective Jones was sitting forward, frowning at me.

"Is something wrong, Mike?" he said.

"She said he had it for as long as she could remember," I said. "But he didn't. Or if he did, he didn't wear it."

"What are you talking about, Mike?" Riel said. He looked a little off balance, like he was still bothered that I hadn't told him who Emily was.

"Nothing." But was it? Was it really nothing? "She said he likes to keep what's his. She said he's got everything tagged and catalogued." Everything he owned — his jewellery, the art on his walls, his books. His kids.

"She?" Detective Jones said.

"Emily."

"What are you trying to say, Mike?"

"The ring Corwin gave Tracie, it was really expensive, right?" I said.

"It was insured for a bundle," Riel said.

"And when Tracie died, it disappeared?"

"All of her jewellery was missing," Detective Jones said.

"Mike, you were there," Riel said. "You heard what Paula said. De la Rivière had it."

"And then he was killed and the ring was never found," I said. "Right?"

"He could have sold it before he died," Detective Jones said.

"He told Paula it was worth a lot to him, remember?" Riel said. I remembered. But I also remembered what Emily had said.

"Emily says her father has this thing about stuff that belongs to him. He had everything identified and tagged and catalogued and insured," I said. I looked at the photograph again.

They were both watching me, waiting again.

"Tracie Howard's ring was stolen when she was murdered. De la Rivière showed it to his girlfriend, but he didn't give it to her. Then James Corwin starts wearing a great big diamond ring on the third finger of his right hand — *after* Tracie is dead," I said.

"Say that again," Riel said.

So I said it again and this time they both looked at the pictures. Detective Jones shook his head. "It's not the same setting."

"He could have taken it to a jeweller and had it put into another setting."

"*If* it's the same diamond," Detective Jones said. "And even if it is, if he was smart, he would have taken it out of the original setting before taking it to a jeweller. If he had taken in the whole ring, we'd have a chance of identifying it. But the diamond alone? Diamonds all look pretty much alike and, as far as I know, you can't positively ID a diamond."

I looked at the ring glinting on James Corwin's finger.

"Actually," I said, "you can."

They both stared at me.

CHAPTER SEVENTEEN

"Another day, another dollar, huh?" Teresa Rego said when I reported for work on Friday night. She was doing her end-of-the-week review of the bulletin board just inside the main doors of the community centre, taking off old announcements and posting new ones. "What would we do without you?"

My community service order had ended a few weeks back, but I was still there, working a couple of hours a day, a couple of days a week and being paid for it. If anyone had told me when I'd started at the community centre that the day would come when I'd actually look forward to filling my bucket with hot water and soap, and that I'd be doing everything the way Mr. Henderson had taught me, even when he wasn't there to make me do it over again, I wouldn't have believed it. But there I was, heading up to the third floor to get started. The only difference was that I had my own key to the utility closets. And, of course, there was another caretaker in charge, a laugh-a-minute young guy who said he was really an actor — a comedic actor — and that he was just doing this until his agent got him some real work. He said, believe it or not, pushing a broom was better than waiting tables. Right. He had been there for two weeks already and I was still waiting to see him with a broom in his hands. It didn't matter to me, though. Teresa knew I was doing a good job. I showed up on time, I did what I was told, and I did it well, the way Mr. Henderson would have.

Besides, it was Friday night. Rebecca was going to meet me after work. We were going to watch videos at her place. Just thinking about walking to her house with her made me feel good all over. Rebecca liked to hold hands. And it was warmer out tonight, so maybe it wouldn't be her mitten in my glove. Maybe it would just be her bare hand in mine. I figured it would be a bump-free night. I figured it would be smooth sailing.

I was wrong.

I finished mopping and started to set up chairs in the big meeting room on the main floor for a recital that was supposed to happen the next day. There were a couple of women at the front of the room going over the arrangements, and another woman over in one corner where the piano was, checking out the music she was going to play. I'd set up maybe half the chairs when I turned around and saw her standing in the doorway. Emily. I hadn't seen her since she'd confronted Mr. Henderson in the basement. She'd been gone by the time I got out of the boiler room. But now here she was, her eyes kind of red, like maybe she'd been crying. But when she zeroed in on me, her whole face pinched and hard and sharp, I knew she wasn't sad. No, she was angry.

"They arrested him," she said.

At first I thought she meant Mr. Henderson,

because they *had* arrested him. They arrested him for holding me in the boiler room, and also on a weapons charge. Riel said he wasn't sure what was going to happen about that, though. He said probably Mr. Henderson did what he did because he couldn't see any reason to go on. First he'd been accused of killing Tracie. Then, by the time he was acquitted, Sarah was in the hospital and Emily was back with her father. And even though he'd been found not guilty, a lot of people still believed that he'd done it and had gotten away with it. James Corwin had made sure of that. Mr. Henderson — Howard — had changed his name, even his appearance, so that people wouldn't look at him or remember his name and think he was a guy who'd got away with murder. Then, after Sarah died, he finally got up his nerve to look for Emily. Riel had to explain to me why Mr. Henderson had all of a sudden resigned from his job.

"The police were looking for him," he said. "He didn't want to go through the accusations all over again."

He also had to explain about the gun. That had really bothered me. As soon as the police showed up, he had pulled a gun on me.

Riel said that when Mr. Henderson had finally seen Emily face to face and she had called him a murderer, it had probably been the last straw. He said he figured Mr. Henderson had hit bottom right then. He said that's probably why he wanted Riel there, to put an end to it once and for all. That's when I remembered what Mr. Henderson had said when he grabbed me. He had said, "Sorry." Riel said there was even a name for it — suicide by cop. Except Riel wasn't a cop anymore. Riel said he was going to see what he could do for Mr. Henderson, see who he could talk to, and maybe the charges against him would be dropped or, at least, he'd get off with a suspended sentence. He said he thought that would be fair.

But when Emily said to me, "They arrested him," she wasn't talking about Mr. Henderson.

"They arrested my father," she said. She yelled the words at me. The two women who were going over the recital arrangements and the woman at the piano all turned to look at her. Emily didn't seem to notice them. "They say he paid a man to kill my mother. They say he killed that man too."

That was news to me. I knew the police were looking into it. Riel had told me. Detective Jones had told him. But I didn't know they had arrested anyone yet.

"I hate you," she said.

Right. Like she had ever actually liked me. Like I even cared.

"If it wasn't for you," she said, "this wouldn't be happening."

At first I thought I'd just keep my mouth shut. What was the point in arguing with her? But when she said that, it got to me.

"The cops found the guy's body," I said. "They figured out who he was. They knew he had your mother's ring after she . . . died." She winced when I mentioned her mother and her eyes got all watery. Well, she had brought up the subject. "Then they found out your father was walking around the whole time, wearing the diamond that had been stolen from her. It didn't have anything to do with me."

Okay, so maybe that wasn't the pure truth. But I had a lot of confidence in the cops. They would have figured it out even if I hadn't said anything. Detective Jones had looked at those photographs. He had made me go over everything I had said. After that, according to Riel, the police had contacted James Corwin's insurance company. They found out that even though Corwin had insured Tracie's ring when he gave it to her, he had never filed a claim when it was stolen. They also found out that he had had it gem-printed — the insurance company had on file a laser print of the diamond that had been in Tracie Corwin's engagement ring. And it turned out that what Emily had told me was true — gemprints were like fingerprints. They'd been successfully used in court to conclusively identify gems. Then the police got a warrant for the ring that James Corwin had been wearing on his finger since a few months after Tracie died, and guess what? It was the same diamond. They tracked down the jeweller who had made the setting, who told them when Corwin had brought it in — a couple of months after Tom Howard was arrested. "You told them things that I told you," she said. "I talked to you and you told the cops and now my dad says it's my fault." Then she did something that really surprised me. Emily Corwin started to cry.

"I'm sorry about your dad," I said. I didn't mean I was sorry he was arrested. I just meant I was sorry she had a dad like that. And I guess I was kind of sorry that she had lost so much — her mother, her sister, and now her father. I wondered what was going to happen to her.

She wiped her tears with the palms of her hands, hard, smearing them, her eyes on me now, angry. "I hate you," she said, screaming at me. One of the women at the front of the room handed the paper she was holding to the woman beside her and started to walk to where we were standing.

"Is everything okay back here?" she said. Her name was Ms Walker. She was a music teacher. I'd seen her work with the kids who were going to be in the recital. She always stayed for a while after they were gone, making notes and going through her music. She always chatted to me too.

"Everything's fine," I said. "Thanks."

I tried to take Emily by the arm, to lead her out of the room, but she wouldn't let me. She stared at me. More tears were running down her face. She stared at me and then she slapped me. Boy, did it ever sting. It took my by surprise too. Ms Walker stepped forward. I saw her open her mouth to say something. Emily turned and walked out of the room.

Ms Walker watched her and then turned to me.

The side of my face was hot. I felt embarrassed. Ms Walker looked at me.

"It's nothing," I said. Except that it wasn't nothing. It was something and I knew exactly what. When my mother died, I was angry. I found excuses to get into fights with kids who still had mothers. After Billy died, I was angry again. I was angry when I was in foster care and I was still angry some of the time after I moved in with Riel. And because I was so angry, I did dumb stuff. So I couldn't say I didn't know. I couldn't say I didn't understand.

"Girlfriend?" Ms Walker said.

I shook my head.

Ms Walker pulled my hand away from my cheek. "Well, she left quite a mark."

* * *

The handprint had faded by the time Rebecca showed up. She kissed me on the same cheek Emily had slapped. Then she slipped her bare hand in mine and we walked over to her house and watched two videos. One was a chick flick, the kind of movie that girls like and that they think are terrific if they get to cry at the end. The other one was an action movie. Rebecca seemed to enjoy it as much as I did.

It was nearly one in the morning by the time I left her house, and past one by the time I got home. Riel was still up when I got there. He was sitting at the kitchen table, smiling down at the tabletop.

"Where's Susan?" She had been at the house when I left for work.

"She's on call. She had to go into work."

Uh-huh. So why the big smile?

"She said yes," he said.

"Yes to . . .?"

"Mike, I'm getting married."

I was happy for him. I really was. But I couldn't help wondering.

"We want you to stay with us, Mike," he said. "We both do. You okay with that?"

I said I was. And, boy, was I ever.

The *Mike and Riel* Series:

Hit and Run

Truth and Lies

Dead and Gone

The *Chloe and Levesque* Series:

Over the Edge

Double Cross

Scared to Death

Break and Enter

No Escape

**Other books by
Norah McClintock:**

Mistaken Identity

The Body in the Basement

Password: Murder

Sins of the Father

*Body, Crime, Suspect:
How a Murder Investigation Really Works*

The *Chloe and Levesque* Series

Over the Edge
Can Chloe figure out who pushed
Adam over the edge?
Red Maple and White Pine
nominee.
$5.99   0-590-24845-6

Double Cross
Finding out what
happened to Jonah's
mother leads Chloe
straight into danger!
$5.99   0-439-98708-3

Scared to Death
What — or *who* — has scared Tessa
to death?
Arthur Ellis Award
$5.99   0-439-98812-8

Break and Enter
Someone is setting
Chloe up . . .
Arthur Ellis Award
$6.99   0-439-98989-2

No Escape
Nobody but Chloe will give Caleb
the benefit of the doubt . . .
White Pine and Manitoba
Young Reader's Choice Nominee
$6.99   0-439-96905-0

The *Mike and Riel* Series

Hit and Run
Was the hit and run accident that killed Mike's mother *really* an accident?
$6.99   0-439-97418-6

Truth and Lies
One little lie leads to another, and ends up making Mike the lead suspect in a *murder* investigation . . .
$6.99   0-439-96919-0

Dead and Gone
The discovery of a long-buried body rekindles a murder investigation that had been unsolved for years . . .
$6.99   0-439-96759-7

Other Exciting Titles

Mistaken Identity

If Zanny's own father isn't
who she thought he was
. . . then who is *she*?
Arthur Ellis Award
$5.99   0-590-24627-5

The Body in the Basement

The body found in Tasha's
parents' café is only the
beginning . . .
Arthur Ellis Award
Winner, Red Maple
Award First Runner-Up
and Manitoba Young
Reader's Choice Award Nominee
$5.99   0-590-24983-5

Sins of the Father

What does Mick have to do to clear his father's name?
Arthur Ellis Award Winner and Red Maple Award Shortlist
$5.99   0-590-12488-9

Password: Murder

Could the clues that Harley discovers mean that his father's death wasn't *really* his fault?
Red Maple Award Shortlist
$5.99   0-590-51505-5

Body, Crime, Suspect: How a Murder Investigation Really Works

Go behind the scenes of a crime case and see how it's solved.
Arthur Ellis Award Nominee
$5.99   0-439-98769-5